Would you like a FREE book and the chance
to win a FREE KINDLE?

Then sign up for the DAN AMES BOOK CLUB:

For special offers and new releases, sign up here

A HARD MAN TO FORGET

THE JACK REACHER CASES

DAN AMES

PRAISE FOR DAN AMES

"Fast-paced, engaging, original."

— NEW YORK TIMES BESTSELLING
AUTHOR THOMAS PERRY

"Ames is a sensation among readers who love fast-paced thrillers."

— MYSTERY TRIBUNE

"Cuts like a knife."

— SAVANNAH MORNING NEWS

"Furiously paced. Great action."

— NEW YORK TIMES BESTSELLING
AUTHOR BEN LIEBERMAN

Copyright © 2017 by Dan Ames

All rights reserved.

Published by Slogan Books, Inc., New York, NY.

A HARD MAN TO FORGET

The Jack Reacher Cases

Book One

Written by Dan Ames

1

The two men with guns walked behind the man carrying the shovel. They knew what they were doing. A shovel was sometimes as good a weapon as any. A man with a shovel and nothing to lose was bound to make an effort with whatever he had.

So they kept their distance.

Should the man turn and swing the shovel with arms extended, his reach would cover eight feet or so.

The men with the guns maintained a ten-foot distance.

The man with the shovel gave no indication of a desire to attack, however. His shoulders were slumped. His feet shuffled along in the sand. He said nothing.

It was night in the desert. The stars were out. The wind was blowing steadily from the southwest but it had no power. It was cool and the men with the guns were chilly. Above them, the night sky was littered with stars.

The man with the shovel was sweating. He trudged along, and his face was slick, glinting in the pale moonlight. Occasionally, he stumbled on a large rock. Without bothering to look at what had impeded his path, he simply moved forward.

The men with the guns neatly avoided the stones the man with the shovel stumbled upon. He was their trailblazer, even though he was the only one who had no idea where they were going.

When the trio was at least a mile from the road, the men with guns glanced at each other, nodded and stopped abruptly.

The man with the shovel initially kept stumbling forward, but eventually, he noticed that his escorts had stopped.

He stopped. Turned and faced them.

One of the men with guns pointed his pistol at a spot on the ground and lifted his chin toward the shovel.

The man with the shovel glanced down at the spot on the ground. He saw nothing special. Sand. Some loose gravel. A weed.

He glanced back up at the men.

They waited.

"You bastards," he said. His words carried no force. No threat. A simple statement, accepted by all.

The man with the shovel put the point of the blade in a spot in front of him. He stepped forward, placed his foot on the shovel and pushed it into the ground.

He started digging.

In the distance a coyote howled. The sound of the steel shovel echoed in the empty desert air. When it hit a loose rock or a layer of gravel, the reverberation seemed to hang in the space above the men.

The men with guns paid no attention to the desert or its distant inhabitants. They were solely focused on the man with the shovel. They continued to keep their distance. A shovel full of sand flung at them was always a possibility. So they stood well back. Close enough to be able to shoot and kill their target with complete confidence, yet far enough to cause a spade full of sand to dissipate over the distance it had to travel.

The man with the shovel showed no signs of a plan to attack.

He was mechanical. Insert shovel. Scoop. Toss sand. Repeat.

His sweating had stopped.

His hands were unsteady. At times, the shovel wobbled in his hands.

It seemed that he was about to say something, but his mouth moved without producing any sound. One of the men with guns was very tall and as he watched the digger's face, it reminded him of a freshly caught fish tossed onto the bank, gasping for air.

When the floor of the desert was level with the middle of the shoveling man's thigh, one of the men with guns spoke. It wasn't the tall one. The other one was short and stocky, with a bull neck.

His voice carried no emotion.

"Toss the shovel. Sit down."

The man in the shallow grave paused. He leaned on the shovel and looked toward the dark purple sky. His lips continued to move, but no sound came out.

One of the men with guns was curious if the

man was praying. But the voice was so soft, and with the ten-foot safety zone, he couldn't hear. But his educated guess was that a prayer was being recited.

The man with the shovel put one hand on the bottom of the tool's handle and threw it into the darkness. It sailed on an arc and rotated slightly, like a perfectly thrown football.

It landed in the sand and made a soft, distant thud.

The man sat down, pulled his knees up toward him and wrapped his arms around them. He buried his face into the space between his arms and his chest.

He was crying.

One of the men with guns stepped forward, lifted his pistol, and fired twice. The pistol was equipped with a silencer and the sound of the shots was little more than a soft *huff*. It made no echo and quickly faded.

The hair on top of the shoveling man's head puffed upward as each bullet entered his skull. He tipped backward and slumped onto his back.

The shooter tilted his head to the side, and judged how well his shots had laid out the man in the grave.

He seemed disappointed with the result.

He unscrewed the silencer and slipped it into a pocket. He placed the gun in a concealed holster underneath his left arm.

He then reached forward and pulled the dead man's feet toward him, so the body was flat in the grave.

The other man retrieved the shovel and joined his partner at the foot of the grave.

He withdrew a quarter from his pocket and let the shovel handle rest against his stomach.

"Call it."

"Heads."

The man with the coin tossed it, caught it and slapped it down on top of his other hand. He then pulled his hand away with a flourish.

He showed it to the other man, who then grabbed the shovel and began tossing sand on top of the dead man.

In the distance, the coyote howled once more.

2

It wouldn't be until much later, long after the bodies had begun to pile up and all hell had broken fully loose, that Lauren Pauling would begin to wonder just why she had been thinking about Jack Reacher that morning.

It had been a fairly routine start to the day.

Early coffee. Quick skim of the New York Times. A brutal workout in the gym housed in the basement of her apartment building. It was a ferocious routine that included a punishing cardio segment followed by an extensive free weight program. As Pauling was nearing the age of fifty, she took special pride in knowing that her fitness regimen would leave much younger women begging for mercy.

A shower, light breakfast and the start of her work day.

For Pauling, that meant leaving her apartment on Barrow Street and heading over to her office on West 4th. As she walked, she glanced at her reflection in the store windows. She was a little taller than average, with goldish blonde hair. Her startling green eyes weren't discernible in the reflection, but they were often the first thing people noticed about her. She could use them strategically when she needed to.

She reached her office building, climbed the narrow staircase, and let herself into the two-room office suite.

There was a casual lounge area at the front with two chairs and a table. Magazines were neatly arranged on the table's surface, and the chairs each held an accent pillow. The walls were home to art prints. Not expensive. Professional.

The second part, her actual office, was in the back.

Pauling was a private investigator. Her top-of-the-line business card gave a little bit more information: Lauren Pauling. Private Investigator. Ex-Special Agent, Federal Bureau of Investigation. At the bottom was an address with 212 and 917 phone numbers for landline and cell, plus e-mail and a website URL.

Like the woman herself, the business card was professional, elegant and direct. The same held true for her website and the office.

It was the picture of efficiency and prestige. Not over-the-top luxurious, but with high-end finishes that would impress clients.

Pauling wasn't cheap.

Her professional habitat reflected that fact.

She cruised through her email with practiced efficiency. Within thirty minutes every issue had been addressed, every necessary action taken, and all inconsequential messages filed.

Maybe it was then, during the momentary lull when her mind turned to Reacher.

Of course, the truth was, it often did.

Pauling's last case with the FBI had been the worst period of her life. A kidnapping turned murder. She had felt like a failure, that she had let the victim down. It wasn't until Jack Reacher arrived that eventually the case of Anne Lane reappeared in her life. Working with Reacher, she'd eventually found justice for Anne.

And then Reacher was gone.

It was his way, she understood that.

But the resulting justice that finally arrived, along with the knowledge that she, Pauling, had done nothing wrong, had breathed new life into her.

She had returned to her company and her career with renewed vigor. As a result, her business had soared to the point where she often turned down work, or referred cases to other investigators.

Now, she shook off thoughts of Reacher.

He was a hard man, and a hard man to forget.

But she had been trying to move on. It just wasn't easy to do. Pauling was well past the point of romantic infatuations. There had been men. Successful. Impressive. Kind.

But none of them had been like Jack Reacher.

And she knew without a doubt that there never would be. There was Jack Reacher, and there was everyone else.

The thought of moving on gave her the motivation to get up from behind her desk, and walk toward her front door. She was going to swing by the mailbox and see if anything had been delivered. She tried not to spend more than a half hour at a time sitting behind her desk. She had a second desk to the right of her main workstation that could be lifted so she could stand and work.

But now, she wanted to move. Thoughts of Reacher always prompted her to take an action of some sort.

As she prepared to leave her office, Pauling spotted a letter that had already arrived, placed neatly under her door.

She hadn't heard anyone stop by.

It was a little early for mail, so she assumed it was an overnight envelope.

But it wasn't.

It was a plain white letter.

With one word emblazoned across its front.

Reacher.

3

D espite having worked for an organization known to have a vague and fluid set of guidelines, Michael Tallon lived by a very specific set of rules.

The saying went that the world was not black-and-white. Plenty of shades of grey, that sort of thing.

While sometimes true, Tallon preferred to live in the black-and-white as much as possible. He detested vague boundaries and shadowy borders. Maybe it was an innate desire to be able to quickly deduce a threat. Split-second decisions between right and wrong. Life and death.

Tallon's mind went to those rules when the man in the restaurant began behaving badly.

It wasn't much of a place, the restaurant. A chain eatery serving generic Mexican food, barely one step up from fast food.

It featured an open seating area, mostly tables separated here and there with a stand of booths. A giant drink dispenser was on one side, the serving counter in the middle, the entrance on the other side. The walls held posters advertising the latest meal special with a soft drink the size of a city's water tower.

A row of plaques touted employees of the month, as well as awards for customer satisfaction, given by the restaurant itself.

The place was half-full, mostly locals, Tallon guessed. His eyes had scanned the customers when he'd entered, and the only person who'd caught his eye was the man now demanding the attention of just about everyone in the place.

"You're a nightmare," the man barked at the young woman sitting across from him. She recoiled at the volume of the man's voice, and the proximity of his face. Tallon figured she probably caught a little spittle on that exclamation.

He tried to ignore the man. He was here only because he was hungry and needed a quick stop before continuing his drive. Tallon had just finished a project and was on his way home.

Ordinarily, he would have pushed through but his need for food had grown to the point of distraction and knew that he still had six hours of driving ahead of him.

He'd ordered the least offensive item on the menu, grilled chicken tacos. The chicken was rubbery, the tortilla soggy. But the coffee was good and surprisingly strong. It was fuel, nothing more.

Tallon had eaten all of the tacos he'd planned to, and was about to take the rest of his coffee and go, when the man's voice cut through the monotonous drone of the restaurant yet again.

"You're worthless, just like your mother," the man said. "Both of you are useless."

All of which brought Tallon's mind around to his rules.

One of which dealt with bad parents.

Tallon had seen his fair share of them and been tempted to intervene on previous occasions. But Tallon believed in perseverance. His own parents had been fair and generous people. But he'd known others who had been cruel and vicious. Yet, he'd seen their children survive and in some cases, even thrive.

The world could be a cold and dark place. At some point, everyone had to learn that donning armor and entering combat was an occasional necessity.

So Tallon had decided not to get involved. The man was big, well over six feet, with greasy hair tied into a ponytail. He wore a sleeveless shirt, revealing thick arms wrapped with barbed wire tattoos.

He had thick hands, with large silver rings on nearly every finger. They looked like skull rings, one of them featured some kind of colored glass pieces for the eyes.

Tallon saw movement to his left and before the older woman rose from her booth, he knew exactly what was going to happen, long before it did.

He'd seen the older couple sitting in the booth near the window. The woman had one of those open, caring faces that denoted a love of family and goodness in others. She also had wide, expressive eyes that revealed an intensity of personality typically seen in someone much younger. It was a face and a demeanor that meant action. This was a woman who preferred to get involved sooner than later.

The man Tallon assumed was the woman's

husband did not share this intensity. He was speaking quietly to the woman and Tallon knew he was urging his wife of many years to not get involved.

She would have none of it.

Tallon watched as the woman crossed the dining area. She had on a pair of blue slacks, a white blouse buttoned up to the neck, and sensible black shoes. She was tall, maybe a former athlete.

A woman of action, Tallon thought.

Most of the humdrum, muted conversations taking place in the restaurant stopped. It seemed to Tallon that even the requisite kitchen noise from behind the service counter had suddenly diminished to a quiet lull.

The older woman arrived at the table of the man and the young girl.

"You're teaching your daughter to accept being abused by a man," the old woman said. "If you continue, she'll look for someone just like you. A thug who berates her and probably beats her. Is that what you want?"

In the background, Tallon saw a worker at the counter dart back into the kitchen, most likely looking for a manager. The old woman's husband began to slide out of his booth. It wasn't a neat, quick move. He wasn't as spry as his wife.

But Tallon knew the big man wasn't going to hesitate. Those rings weren't for display. The guy was a brawler. He had it written all over his face, and his hands.

"Fuck off, you old bitch," the big man roared. He lunged to his feet and the old woman retreated halfway back to her husband. They collided, and the woman fell to the floor.

"No, Dad! Leave her alone," the young girl screamed. Her face had turned red and she had started to cry. It was terror that had given her the courage to talk. And a compassion for someone other than herself. Her father had probably beaten down the ability to care for herself, but the inherent goodness was still there, as long as it was reserved for others.

But the big man wasn't listening.

He moved quickly toward the woman and her husband.

Tallon noted the big man's dirty blue jeans and his thick, black leather steel-toed boots. He was walking toward the woman and Tallon knew with utmost certainty that he planned to punch and then stomp the woman before she got to her feet. He'd probably try to clobber the old husband, too.

Had to impress his daughter, his pea brain probably told him.

Tallon's rules about bad parents were one thing.

Innocent bystanders were a whole different ballgame. There were no blurry lines on that one.

He was out of his booth and between the big man and the older couple before anyone had a chance to react.

Tallon was face-to-face with the big man.

"Turn around, go back and apologize to your daughter," Tallon said.

The man laughed, his face incredulous. He looked behind him, wondering, Tallon supposed, if a bevy of cops had suddenly arrived to supply backup.

But there was no one. Just a scared girl and a restaurant staff all peering out from behind the counter with blank stares.

Tallon read the story that was on the man's face. A cruel man, wanting to prove his superiority, and single-handedly destroy everyone who got in his path, in a little chain restaurant on the outskirts of nowhere, U.S.A.

The eyes changed, turned almost gleeful, and Tallon knew the punch was on its way before the big man even did.

The man's blow was slightly unorthodox, slow, but with a fair amount of power behind it.

Rather than avoid it, Tallon simply stepped into it, deflected the arm wide, caught it in both hands and slammed it down on the back of one of the restaurant's fixed chairs.

The arm snapped like a medium-sized piece of driftwood.

The man screamed and staggered, almost falling to his knees.

Tallon drove his elbow into the man's throat, cutting off the scream, and then as the man continued to drop, followed it with a knee to the face. Tallon both felt and heard the cartilage squish like fresh roadkill beneath a truck tire.

The man's eyes rolled back into his head.

Behind them, the manager disconnected from a call he had just made. 9-1-1, Tallon knew.

He had just enough time, so he began pulling the rings from the man's fingers.

He wasn't sure why, exactly.

A part of him recognized the rings were old, and that the man's fingers had grown fat around them. They were the man's armor. Something about the way they had looked made Tallon feel like the man got some kind of special confidence from them. And had felt that way for a long time.

So they didn't come off easily.

One pulled most of the skin off the finger it was attached to.

Tallon had to break three fingers to get the accompanying rings free.

With all of the rings now in his right hand, he forced them into the man's mouth, breaking several teeth in the process.

Tallon then returned to his table, took his tray and slid the plate and remaining food into the waste bin. He took an extra napkin and wiped off his hands.

He walked over to the young girl and pulled out a wad of cash from his front pocket. He guessed there was nearly a thousand dollars there. Using his body to shield the view of the man on the ground even though he was completely unconscious, he handed the girl the money.

"Get on a bus. Take your Mom if she loves you. Get out of here. He probably didn't learn the lesson."

The girl mumbled something soft but she slipped the money into her pocket and stood to leave.

With a nod to the old couple, Tallon left.

He still had a six-hour drive ahead of him.

4

Miles from the dead man who'd been forced to dig his own grave, another project was being undertaken.

This, too, was being performed under the cover of darkness, with only modest lighting required.

The coyote who had serenaded the dead man during his execution was now nowhere to be found.

Instead, the same two men with guns were now present, along with a half-dozen others.

The activity took place behind a gated entrance off a dirt road in the middle of the desert, surrounded by razor wire and signs proclaiming private property. There were a half-dozen buildings, spread out in the style of a quasi-military complex. The biggest of the structures was the size of an airplane hangar.

Bundles of desert camouflage netting were littered throughout the complex, some in place, others waiting to be utilized as circumstances arose.

Unlike their activity hours earlier, the two men with guns were not burying a human being.

This time, a large piece of machinery was slowly making its way into a new home.

Underground.

In the large, hangar-like building, a huge retractable door was raised, revealing a tunnel the width of three traffic lanes. Everything was painted military gray, and the path was illuminated with lights protected by metal screens.

There was some hushed talking, subtle yet unmistakable hand gestures being made, and a delicate job was in the process of precise completion. The air smelled of gasoline, motor oil and fresh paint.

Near the back of the hangar, a man stood silently. He was very tall. Very thin. With a bald head that caught the harsh light of the hangar's interior. The men working did not look at him directly, instead, they seemed to note his presence in their peripheral vision.

Once the large item was securely deposited and the huge door rolled back into place, the bald man turned and entered an elevator with buttons showing two floors beneath ground level.

He entered the elevator and pressed the button for the lowest level.

Outside, the lights of the complex were shut off and the camouflage netting was moved into place by an automated system, like a football stadium with a retractable roof.

In the dark, with the netting in place, the entire structure was nearly invisible.

Along the dirt road, the tire tracks from the vehicles were slowly being erased by the night's desert wind.

5

Wen the situation demanded it, Lauren Pauling could move with a quickness and agility that often surprised the people around her. Her fast-twitch muscle fibers were always primed, and her reflexes as well as her endurance were a bit of a legend at the Bureau.

Her preference, however, was to always proceed when possible with deliberation.

Survey. Analyze. Intuit.

Which is how she handled the arrival of the mysterious white envelope.

The one that simply read *Reacher.*

She stood still in her office, her head cocked

slightly to one side as she ran a series of rapid observations and calculations through her mind.

Definitely not delivered by the mail.

Too early.

Definitely not delivered via one of the overnight services as the envelope was plain, with no labels bearing the name of a shipping company.

She also rapidly discounted the notion that it had been incorrectly delivered to another address and brought to her office by the resident of the wrong address.

There was no address at all on the front.

Nor was her name included.

All of which told Pauling that the letter had been hand-delivered.

A courier, maybe.

Still, most couriers had instructions on whether or not to obtain proof of delivery. In the majority of cases, that was the norm.

Which meant if the envelope had been brought by courier, the instructions had been to simply deliver the envelope without obtaining a signature.

Why?

Had the courier been told not to be seen? To

simply slide the letter under the door and disappear?

Pauling took a step closer to the mysterious guest on the floor of her office.

Living in New York, the favorite target of various terrorists groups, tended to make a person suspicious of generic packages being delivered. And Pauling was no exception.

Added to that, she was ex-FBI and had performed her share of duties involving foreign enemies of the state.

If that weren't enough, she and Jack Reacher had done some serious damage to a crooked mercenary. Maybe one of his gang was back and wanted revenge.

Pauling discounted that as well.

Even a letter bomb would have some kind of shape.

This was slim. Pauling guessed it held one piece of paper. Probably not even a full sheet. Notecard sized.

Pauling also ruled out the notion that Jack Reacher had delivered the message. Not Reacher's style. He was direct and to the point. Yes, he moved around the country anonymously, but there was no way he would have arrived at her door and dropped off a piece of paper without announcing his presence.

Pauling had gathered all of this intelligence by assessing the front side of the envelope only. Now she stepped forward, leaned down and turned the letter over before picking it up.

There was nothing on the back.

That, too, confirmed her previous theories.

A hand-delivered letter.

She picked it up, brought it to her desk and set it before her. She sat down. Leaned forward. Smelled the envelope.

Only the vague smell of paper, a kind of unimpressive scent one associated with a tiny copy room in a corporation. Or an office supply store when it first receives its shipments of back-to-school supplies.

A trace of New York car exhaust as well.

That was it.

Deciding she had gathered all of the information she could, Pauling used a letter opener and sliced the envelope open.

One slip of paper eased itself out onto her desk.

It was notecard sized.

Folded in half.

No fancy trim. Or bold lettering. Or heavy linen stock.

Just a garden-variety notecard.

Pauling opened it.

Written in black ink with a firm hand, was a phone number.

The number meant nothing to her.

6

Nearly two thousand miles from the mysterious activity in the desert, a group of people assembled around a large table made of a dark wood polished to perfection. It was nearly black, and reflected the recessed lighting above, as well as the anguished faces seated around its perimeter.

There were file folders on the table. Laptops with multiple wires running into neatly camou-flaged openings. Paper cups filled with industrial-strength coffee.

Very few words were spoken.

A large screen at one end of the room displayed a satellite map. There were no cities listed. No roads with electronic labels attached. Any clearly delineated location was absent.

What little activity was taking place stopped when the door opened and a man entered.

He was older than most, but with square shoulders, a neat buzz cut, and a posture that implied confidence, assertiveness and total command.

Without hesitation, he walked to the head of the table. He looked down at the chair, but chose to stand. He appraised the various men and women seated around the table.

He spoke in a clipped manner, with a timbre that betrayed authority.

"I want the person in the room with most current information to tell me in as few words as possible..." he said.

His eyes went from person to person before he finished the thought.

"...just what in the hell is going on."

7

D eath was home to Michael Tallon.

The small town of Independence Springs was nestled in the south-western crook of Death Valley.

It was situated between Los Angeles and Las Vegas, in an area most people saw from the very distant highway.

Tallon owned a decent-sized chunk of land and a small adobe house. Some referred to it as a casita. Others, a ranch.

To Tallon, it wasn't a home. He thought of it as headquarters.

From the outside, it appeared to be a typical California gentleman's ranch. Someone who might prefer to play cowboy on the weekends. Or the kind of home a retired couple who couldn't afford the lavish homes of a bigger city might turn to for a warm and low-cost option.

Because of Tallon's background, the home had some interesting features.

Multiple security cameras. An alarm system with two backup generators. An armory. A weightlifting room that occupied the entire garage. A landscape that appeared to be ordinary, but was in fact strategically laid out to prevent cover for an attacking force while also providing advantageous shooting lanes for someone inside the structure.

Likewise, the home's electronics were significantly out of the ordinary. There was a hardwired landline. A wireless radio unit. Two satellite phones with multiple batteries and chargers. A hardwired communication system for cable and Internet, along with a satellite-based stream that could continue to feed the home information without power and if the physical cables were somehow severed.

The windows were bulletproof, the entry doors made of specific construction designed to withstand explosives and fire.

One might assume Michael Tallon was a man with a great deal of enemies.

While that was true, it was also true that most of them were dead.

Still, Tallon had taken some precautions because he could afford to, and it made more sense to install fortifications than to skimp.

When he did things, Tallon tried to do them the right way.

Now, he disarmed the security system, walked through the house and satisfied with the results, unloaded his gear. He stashed his weapons, showered, and splashed a finger's worth of whiskey into a glass.

He sat in the living room, with the picture window looking out over the broad expanse of desert to the mountains beyond. The interior of the room was darker than the outside, and a film of reflective material adorned the exterior. No one could see in, but Tallon could see out.

It was good to be back, he thought.

His project had been completed with neat efficiency, and all had gone as planned.

Except for the confrontation in the restaurant.

Tallon's mind went to the young girl. She had a challenge in front of her, that was for certain. The police would come. They would do a half-hearted search for the man who had injured the original assailant. But they wouldn't find anything. Tallon was quite gifted when it came to leaving no trace of his presence.

But the girl. He hoped she would take his money and leave. Find a friend. Or a family member. Maybe her Mom wasn't so bad. Maybe they just needed a break.

Maybe consider the intervention of a stranger a sign to forge a new path.

He hoped so.

But it was a guarded kind of hope. He wished he had a way to follow up, but he knew he couldn't. To have given the girl any kind of information would have been a mistake. She would have been forced to give the same information to the police, and then there would be issues.

He had done the right thing.

But a part of him wondered...had he done enough?

8

The deliberations continued.

Pauling had lunch with a contact at the United Nations. She was a woman, too. She and Pauling had a professional relationship. But they recognized in each other the same trials and tribulations that always came with being a strong and intelligent woman in the world.

Their friendship had benefits.

Pauling sometimes used the woman for information. Information she couldn't get from her regular contacts at the Bureau. Or the State Department. Or even her databases for which she paid significantly large sums of money every month.

There simply was no substitute sometimes for boots on the ground.

It was something she knew Jack Reacher strongly believed in as well.

The woman from the UN also received benefits. Mostly career advice and world experience. The woman from the UN spoke multiple languages, had traveled far and wide but not in the same circles that Pauling had traveled in. Therefore, she often used Pauling as a sounding board. Pauling's analytical mind was razor-sharp and the woman had recognized a resource when she saw it.

For Pauling, lunch was delightful. A refreshing break. A wonderful salad of field greens, candied walnuts and smoked salmon. With a glass of sparkling water. And excellent, thought-provoking conversation.

In the back of her mind, however, Pauling was thinking about the phone number and the mysterious envelope with Reacher's name on it.

Pauling loved mysteries. And puzzles. It was why she had gone into law enforcement in the first place.

She'd always enjoyed challenges, and so she'd made a career out of them. The more complex the task, the better.

After lunch Pauling walked back to her office. It was a sunny day in New York, the shadows of the buildings diminished the warmth, but Pauling stayed in the sun when she could. Most of the office dwellers were back at their desks and the sidewalks were relatively light with foot traffic. It was one of the pleasures of being self-employed. The opportunity to set one's own schedule and guarantee a moment, here and there, to relax.

In her office, Pauling got behind her desk and opened one of her databases. She used a reverse lookup service and searched for information on the mystery number.

The results were immediate.

It was a cell phone.

Registered to someone in Albuquerque, New Mexico.

That was interesting.

Pauling had never been to Albuquerque. She'd been to Las Cruces, New Mexico to chase a drug dealer who'd slipped into the country near El Paso. Eventually, she'd caught him near the Mescalero Indian Reservation hiding in a dilapidated RV being driven by a pair of eighty-year-old hippies.

But she'd never been to Albuquerque. Her mind instantly went to Reacher. His travels took him everywhere, she knew. Had he been in Albuquerque? Had he sent the message from there to her office in New York?

For a moment, she wondered if Reacher needed help.

And then she laughed at herself over the silliness of that thought.

Reacher never needed anyone's help, as far as she knew.

Still, the question of the envelope was a puzzle, and she was enjoying the diversion.

Finally, she decided the time for contemplation was over.

Pauling picked up her phone, punched in the numbers and waited for a voice at the other end of the line.

9

The prisoner's IQ was in the low-rent neighborhood of 75 or so. Five points below the lowest end of the average spectrum of human intelligence.

IQ and personality are not intertwined, however.

His antisocial and sociopathic tendencies had originated all on their own. They weren't caused by his low mental capacity; rather, they were exposed by it.

In other words, his innate nature fated him to a life of crime. His diminished intelligence guaranteed he would be caught. And quickly.

By the time the day's test subject was fifteen, he had been incarcerated multiple times. Upon his latest release, he had been sentenced to a halfway house. Adding to his repertoire of less than savory characteristics, he soon included addiction.

Heroin, to be exact.

An offer of free drugs led to his abduction, and he now found himself strapped to a straight-backed wooden chair whose legs were bolted to the concrete floor.

The room was all concrete, with a single over-head light, and a pipe that ran the length of the wall, up to the ceiling, to an austere shower head, poised directly over the test subject's head.

The prisoner had a strange intuition that he was underground. Maybe it was the quality of the acoustics. Or the lack of windows. Or the slightly damp, musty smell. Like a basement.

Behind a thick window made of one-way glass, a small group watched the prisoner. They observed him with great interest. They each held a clipboard with a sheet filled with lines and boxes meant to be utilized once the experiment began.

Standing at the rear of the group was a bald man of impressive stature. He stood nearly six and a half feet tall, with broad shoulders and a face comprised of razor-sharp angles. The man's head was shaved, revealing several blood vessels protruding with great visibility. His eyes were clear and blue, and a little wider than normal as if he was either mildly surprised, or watching the world around him with great intensity.

Those who knew him well, knew it was the latter.

They also knew his blood vessels were dilated for a reason. He was both a medical doctor as well as a doctor of philosophy. His medical degree allowed him a large amount of latitude in prescribing himself unusual and unique pharmaceutical products designed to increase his musculature, as well as his intellect.

The physical side effects were all too apparent.

The psychological ramifications were not.

The group in front of the man had no intention of making their observations known, however. They were solely focused on the prisoner on the other side of the wall. Each and every one of them knew as well that the man behind them was observing *them*, as much as the unfortunate victim strapped to the chair. They much preferred to be observed in their current setting than in the space on the other side of the protected wall.

Somewhere behind them a mechanical thunk reverberated throughout the room. As a group, they all straightened in their chairs and moved their pens into position over their papers. The man at the rear of the room remained immobile.

A gurgling sound echoed throughout the space, followed by a hiss and then from the shower head a stream of muddy brown liquid sprang, showering down on the prisoner below.

The man struggled against his straps, but to no avail. They were industrial-grade and impossible for a human being of even superhuman strength to break. The chair itself was extremely sturdy and could withstand any amount of panicked torque.

The man in the chair bucked and heaved, screamed and cursed. Initially, they were protestations of fear, however, as the liquid continued to rain down upon the man, his skin turned red and blisters began to appear. The fear turned to anger, followed by hostile shouting and cursing. Gradually, his voice lost volume and his throat and vocal cords burned.

His head slumped forward.

The liquid continued to pour down onto his now inert form.

Soon, the effects on his body would be severe and irreversible.

Behind the wall, the people with the clipboards began to write.

The man at the back of the room leaned forward.

He was smiling.

10

"Hello?"

The voice on the other end of the line belonged to a woman. Voices were always difficult to assess age, but Pauling guessed the woman was younger. Somewhere between mid-twenties and mid-thirties.

"Hello, this is Lauren Pauling, I'm a private investigator. With whom am I speaking?"

"Who? Who are you?"

The woman sounded exasperated and harried. In the background, Pauling could hear the sound of other voices and possibly someone typing on a keyboard.

Pauling answered by speaking a little more slowly, and a tad louder. "Lauren Pauling, I'm a private investigator. Someone delivered a letter to me with this phone number."

"Hold on," the woman said.

Pauling listened and heard the swish of fabric, which probably meant the woman had placed the phone against herself. Most likely, the woman was at work, in an office, and needed to go somewhere private to take the call.

Moments later, Pauling heard the sound of a door closing and the woman came back on the line.

"Okay," the woman said.

Pauling waited but the woman apparently had no intention of precipitating conversation.

"First off, did you send me this letter?" Pauling asked.

"No, I didn't send any letter to anyone." Her voice was guarded. As if she was being questioned by an authority figure.

"Okay," Pauling said. "Are you in need of a private investigator for any reason?"

Silence on the other end of the line. There was the vague sound of traffic and Pauling figured the woman had left her office building and was now taking the call outside, which seemed a little extreme.

Why the need for such intense privacy?

"Hello?" Pauling asked.

"I'm here," the woman said.

"Do you know a Jack Reacher?" Pauling asked.

"Who?"

"Jack Reacher."

"No."

A prank, Pauling thought. *It had to be a prank.* Someone must have read about her exploits with Reacher on the Anne Lane case. Why they would have gone to the trouble of doing something as annoying and petty as this was beyond the realm of her imagination. But stranger things had happened.

Still, the behavior of the woman on the other end of the line was odd. Usually, a prank had some sort of punchline.

So far, there was nothing.

Well, she had work to do. If no one needed her help, she was happy to move on to the next task for the day.

"I'm sorry," Pauling said. "There must have been some mistake. I sincerely apologize for the intrusion–"

There was a muffled sound and Pauling stopped talking.

She listened intently.

The sound came again.

Had the woman gasped?

"Hello?" Pauling asked.

Another sound.

And then Pauling realized what she was hearing.

The woman was crying.

11

The man in charge of the group of people seated around the big black conference table went by the name of Rollins. He had a first name. And a fairly impressive title. But he preferred to be called Rollins. Nothing more. Nothing less.

He waited patiently while the individuals around the table weighed their response to his request for someone to tell him what the hell was going on.

However, Rollins knew they weren't just organizing their thoughts before speaking, they were also assessing their competitive rank in the room.

The lower a person's rank in the hierarchy, the less need there was to speak. Those with laptops vacillated between peering intently at their screen, while also trying to acknowledge the boss had just issued a statement someone in the room needed to address.

The longer the silence went on, the more charged the air in the room became.

Eventually, barely perceptible shifts in body language had everyone leaning slightly toward the man centrally seated along the edge of the table.

His name was Petrie.

Unlike the square shouldered, silvery buzz cut presence of Rollins, Petrie was a small man. He had a head that was very narrow, as if someone had squeezed it together like a loaf of bread being pinched between firmer items in the grocery cart. His nose was long, with a high Roman arch. His eyes were set back in his head.

The effect was that of a small predatory bird.

"Since the initial notification, we have been gathering data. That process continues. It's still too early to draw any conclusions," Petrie finally said.

"Please state your early conclusions," Rollins said. It was a rebuke. Stalling was not acceptable. Theories needed to be formulated. Hypotheses tested. Insights discovered.

The room lapsed into silence.

Rollins swiveled his head slowly, letting his gaze fall on every individual for at least a few seconds.

Finally, it settled on a woman seated last at the table. She had short, auburn hair cut into a hip wedge shape. Her face was guileless, but it was the kind of openness that held an advantage. Many had trusted the countenance, only to discover that it had been a tripwire.

She lifted her head, taking her gaze from the laptop in front of her and fastening her eyes directly onto Rollins.

"Someone is so far ahead of us we can't even see their taillights," she said.

12

The sun was merciless, but mercy was the last thing Tallon wanted.

His goal was punitive in nature. What didn't kill you made you stronger.

He began the run with a sprint, to break the sweat and to jump start his heart rate. There was a trail that meandered from a canyon entrance several miles from his house. He had driven there, parked, and embarked on his training run.

What was he training for?

He often asked himself that question. He was training for any eventuality, he told himself. The unexpected. The upcoming. The unforeseen enemy around the corner.

It was his way of life.

He'd been taught that reflexes came down to training. When presented with split-second decisions, under duress, most individuals reverted to their most basic instincts. In other words, in order for the desired behavior to occur, it had to be second nature. And it could only become that deeply ingrained through repeated training. Over and over and over. Until a person did it without thinking.

Because in the heat of battle, there usually wasn't time for intellectualizing.

A person reacted quickly, or they died.

It was that simple.

Tallon wore a weighted vest to simulate a pack or a weapon. He wore a lightweight T-shirt, camouflage cargo pants, hiking boots, a baseball cap and sunglasses. On his wrist was a multifunction watch. On the inside of his pants was a concealed holster with a 9mm pistol. Opposite the pistol was a folding knife, honed to a razor edge.

Once his breath was coming in gasps, Tallon slowed the pace to a steady jog, one that would eat up the miles and that he could maintain for hours. It was his default pace.

The canyons were rimmed with red, the sand a dirty brown that showed darker where the wind or an animal had disturbed the ground. An occasional field mouse darted out of Tallon's way and overhead a hawk was watching his progress.

Routine was never a good thing. Tallon knew that patterns were bad. As a hunter, he had used them extensively himself. On days like this, Tallon never took the same route twice, but he had a general idea in mind for the length of the run. He usually aimed for around ten miles and by alternating his choices to avoid uneven terrain, he was able to not only vary his path but extend or shorten the distance based on his current preference.

Today was a longer day.

All of the time on the road, trapped in a vehicle had left him restless and irritable. The open desert calmed him. The extremes of nearby Death Valley helped him maintain his perspective and focus.

As he ran, the calm that so often quickly arrived on these excursions failed to materialize. He was off. Something felt foreign to him.

His eyes and mind sought out differences in the surrounding terrain. Maybe there was someone else out in the desert. Hikers. Campers. Meth manufacturers. It wouldn't be the first time he'd come across others seeking refuge in the desert, for various reasons.

But he saw no one.

Tallon continued on.

The hawk had left his holding pattern and was gone. A snake crossed Tallon's path a hundred yards ahead.

His stride ate up the miles and less than ninety minutes later, he was nearing the completion of his route.

Tallon was satisfied with his performance.

But the outing had left him troubled.

As if he had missed something.

Something out there in the desert.

13

"Who are you?" the woman asked. "I know you said your name. But, like, who are you? Really?" She sniffled. Her voice trembled and Pauling knew the effort to utter even those words had been significant.

Pauling gave the woman a moment and then said, "My name is Lauren Pauling. I'm a private investigator based in New York City. Your phone number was delivered to my office via a letter."

"I don't understand," the woman said.

"Why don't we start with your name?" Pauling said. She had a fresh pad of paper in front of her, her pen ready to start writing.

"I don't know," the woman said.

"You don't know your name?"

"No, I mean I don't know if I should talk to you. I don't know what to do." The woman's voice had risen in tone, and Pauling knew she was about to burst into tears. Probably trying to keep it in check since she would have to go back to her desk. A face ruined by tears would be noticed by coworkers.

The young woman was desperately trying to keep it together.

"Why are you afraid to tell me your name?" Pauling asked.

"Yes. I mean. I'm afraid to talk to you. I don't know who you are or why you're calling me. I don't know if it's some kind of trick. Or a test. I just don't know."

The woman's voice had grown softer, to almost a whisper. She was panicked. Scared.

Pauling tried to be as soothing as possible. "Look, why don't we start over. First, tell me if you're in any immediate danger."

A long pause and then, "I don't know."

Pauling idly tapped the end of the pen against the sheet of paper. It was the only sound in the office. Tap. Tap. Tap.

A thought occurred to her.

"Are you worried someone is listening to this phone call?"

The woman gasped. Pauling took that as confirmation.

"Do you have children?" Pauling asked.

"No."

"Are you married?"

"Yes," the woman said, but the answer triggered another round of sobbing.

Pauling patiently waited for the woman to catch her breath.

"Did something happen to your husband?"

"I don't...know," the woman choked out. "I can't do this. Can't talk. On the phone. I have to go. They're going to wonder where I am."

The thought occurred to Pauling that she could simply leave the woman her phone number and tell her to call her if she felt like she needed help. Ordinarily, she would have given serious consideration to going in that direction.

Leaving the matter in someone else's hands.

Except for one thing.

Reacher.

The name had been on the envelope. Why? Who had written it? Clearly not this woman. She was scared of her own shadow. Plus, she claimed she'd never heard the name Jack Reacher.

Pauling had gotten to know Reacher very well. She recognized in him an almost pathological need to fight for the little guy. The innocent being victimized by those in power abusing their position.

Was this woman one of those people?

Was Reacher unable to help this woman and so somehow had managed to send a message to Pauling?

Too many questions.

No answers whatsoever.

"According to your cell phone number, you live in the Albuquerque area?" Pauling asked.

"Yes."

"Is there a safe place we can meet? A public place?"

"Probably. I mean, yes. There's my office. Where I work."

Pauling ran through the time it would take her to get to the airport, and her best guess at flights out of New York.

"Okay, I tell you what," Pauling said. She hesitated for just a moment, a little surprised at herself for reaching the decision she was about to make. "I'm going to get on a plane, and come out and see if I can help you. If I can, great. If not, no harm done."

"Umm," the woman said.

"I'll try to get there late tonight if possible. If not, first thing in the morning."

"It's just that–"

"Just what?"

Another long pause and then the woman whispered.

"I think they're coming for me, too."

14

The prisoner with the low IQ looked down at the mess on the floor. Blood. But with something mixed in. He kept looking at it, but nothing registered. It felt oddly familiar yet totally foreign.

And then he realized what it was.

His hair.

Almost all of it. Most of it had come off in small chunks, literally melting from his head like an ice dam in a river finally breaking up in the spring.

Along with the hair there were several chunks of skin.

He screamed, or at least he thought he did, but he couldn't hear anything. Great waves of red and yellow lights flashed in his eyes. His skin was on fire. Pressure from within his skull made him feel like his eyes were going to burst from their sockets.

He'd known pain before.

But nothing like this.

He'd inflicted pain on others. Some of their faces flashed across his consciousness. There was the first woman he'd ever attacked. A former friend he'd nearly beaten to death. That, too, had been an attack he'd started. A cowardly blow from behind with a hammer.

The screams in his mind echoed the screams that struggled to escape his burned throat and mouth.

He couldn't tell which agony was real and which were memories.

With a lunge, his body surged against his restraints, but to no avail.

He was trapped.

And he was dying.

Like every other time in his life when he had desperately needed someone, anyone, there had been no one.

It was up to him

If he couldn't help himself, then there was no help at all.

Another light flashed before his eyes, but this

one was different. It didn't register with him as one associated with pain.

He wondered if it was God.

He'd been to church as a kid, before all of the troubles began, and he wondered if he'd died and was going to see Jesus. Or heaven. Or maybe it was hell. Maybe he had died and this was hell.

There had been no doubt in his mind that he would not be going to heaven. Then again he had stopped believing in God a long time ago. So it didn't really matter.

All he knew was that this kind of pain was pure hell.

The real kind.

More pain, this time in his arm and his neck. Sharp, stabbing pain.

He recognized the sensation, even his full-throated agony.

Needles.

They were sticking needles into him.

15

Pauling flew first class, one of the perks of owning her own business. There was no one in accounting to question her spending.

The buck stopped with her.

When she had been a young FBI agent, on the government dime, accommodations had usually been less than premium. Despite public perception of government agencies being extravagant spenders - $800 toilet seats, anyone? – they had always been conscious of the fact they were funded by taxpayer dollars. So usually they were on the cheapest flights, in the worst hotel rooms, with the shoddiest rental cars. And with an extremely low per diem for meals, restaurants were usually fast and cheap.

As a private investigator, a successful one at that, Pauling had become extremely well-versed in the business aspect of expense reporting and tax deductions.

Now, she insisted on first-class flights, and first tier hotels. Rental cars she didn't care about. And she still usually opted for quick, healthy meals.

After the plane took off and they leveled at altitude, Pauling took out her laptop, connected to her paid in-flight Wi-Fi account, and launched her browser.

After a lot of teeth-pulling and crying, she had been able to get the woman's name in Albuquerque.

It was Cassady Simmons.

Cassady with an 'a' the woman had told her.

Now, Pauling began to search for what she could find out about the mystery woman who had some connection to Reacher, and appeared to be in a great deal of trouble.

Or, more accurately, in a great deal of fear.

Whether or not that anxiety had any basis in reality, Pauling was about to find out.

There was scant information on Cassady

Simmons. The only social media account she had was a Facebook profile marked private. No way to hack around that. Pauling was able to look up tax records and parse through them, until she came to a Cassady Simmons who was married to a Rick Simmons. Their ages were 29 and 31, respectively. They had purchased a house two years ago. There was no employment information on paper, but Cassady had given Pauling her work address. It was for a supply company, Pauling discovered backtracking from the address, and it looked like a fairly mundane operation.

She continued to search, but could find little else.

Pauling closed her laptop and thought about the potential of what she might find. The flight went quickly, and she got up once to stretch her legs, use the restroom, and work out the kinks in her neck from sitting so long. Business travel was never the glamorous enterprise so often portrayed in the media or in films.

She got back to her seat and her thoughts inevitably turned to Jack Reacher. The thought had occurred to her that she might see him in Albuquerque. Maybe he had taken on Cassady Simmons' case and needed her help. She caught herself again. Jack Reacher was a one-man army who never called for backup.

And Pauling was too realistic to think that he simply wanted to see her again.

No, there was something else going on in Albuquerque.

Cassady Simmons either was in trouble, or for some reason deeply believed she was in some sort of danger.

Pauling was slightly torn. On the one hand, she hoped this woman wasn't in any kind of trouble. On the other hand, that would mean she would be wasting the better part of two days flying back and forth across the country.

The plane eventually reached its destination and after a smooth landing, Pauling hit the terminal, heading fast for the rental car shuttle.

It was time to meet Cassady Simmons.

16

"Who do we have out there?" Rollins asked the group.

They were still sitting around the long, black table. They'd been at it for hours and fatigue had set in. Irritability. Answers had become more clipped. Impatient.

"The SAC is Ray Ostertag," said Petrie, the small man with the hooked nose. "He's a good man. But obviously the initial call came to us because of the potential situation."

"Ostertag's qualifications," Rollins stated.

"He's a good man," Petrie continued. His voice had become more enthusiastic, reflecting his satisfaction in being able to supply an answer. Even if it was to something fairly mundane like the qualifications of the people underneath him. "Ostertag spent a lot of time in Chicago working gangs. Also a fair amount of intelligence background."

"Good, he may need it," Rollins said.

He shifted his attention from Petrie and looked around the room.

His gaze settled briefly on the woman who'd made the comment about the taillights. He moved on from her and once again landed on Petrie. The others around the table again shifted slightly in their chairs, waiting for what came next.

Just as Petrie was about to offer a suggestion, Rollins spoke, cutting him off.

"Agent Hess," Rollins said. The woman seated last at the table lifted her gaze.

"Sir," she answered.

"Get out there. Assess the situation. Report back to us within twenty-four hours."

Without waiting for a reply, he turned to Petrie.

"You need to have a full threat assessment on my desk by noon tomorrow. I want every possibility researched with specific counter measures and damage estimates. This has the potential to get out of control fast. We can't let that happen."

He left the room.

Petrie looked at Hess. "We'll give Ostertag a

heads up. The minute you're there and have done an initial download, call me. Tell me what they've got, what they can and can't do, and what you need."

Hess closed her laptop and stood.

"Will do," she said.

17

Pauling's rental car was a white Impala. A big, roomy four-door. Some habits died hard. She'd spent so many hours riding in and driving the Lincoln Town Cars that she was simply used to the size.

Now, she let it cruise down the freeway toward Albuquerque. Cassady Simmons had told her that she worked for a company called Industrial Supply & Wholesale. According to Google, it was on the south side of the city, on the other side of the Rio Grande.

Pauling always marveled at cities of this size. About a million people if you included the suburbs.

Cities of this size were always nice. Very

contained. Being a frequent traveler, she always enjoyed the smaller airports which tended to be cleaner and much faster to get through.

Albuquerque also enjoyed a picturesque setting. The mountains in the background, shouldering shadows down to the banks of the big river. It was easy to see why someone had stopped here and decided to stay.

Pauling recognized that she liked the feel of a smaller city, but wasn't fooling herself. She was a big fan of New York. It was her home.

The allure of going somewhere smaller, cheaper, and more accessible was understandable. Pauling had no real hometown to speak of. Her father had been in the military and they'd traveled far and wide. It was probably the military life that had nudged her toward the Bureau, a quasi-military operation. And maybe it explained why she'd had such a powerful attraction to Jack Reacher.

It took Pauling less than twenty minutes to reach Industrial Supply & Wholesale's office. It was a brick building, cream-colored, that looked like it was at least fifty years old. Probably part warehouse with a section that had been converted into offices.

The area in general was a warehouse district

that appeared to be at the beginning of some gentrification attempts. Sandwiched in around the warehouses were converted factory buildings that now housed condos. On one corner, she saw a brewpub and an organic coffee shop. Maybe the gentrification was further along than she'd first reckoned.

Pauling found a parking spot a block from the office building and eased the Impala into its space. She left the car running with the air conditioning on. It was hot. It was time to get ready to meet Cassady Simmons.

Pauling got out of the car, went to the trunk, and opened her lone suitcase. She had supplied all of the necessary permits to check her handgun. Now, she retrieved the case and brought it back into the car in the front seat, opened it, and removed her gun. She loaded it, cocked and locked it, and slipped it into a holster on her left hip.

Next, she retrieved a small notebook and pen from her briefcase and looked at her phone. She had added Cassady as a contact and sent her a text. They had agreed to meet on Cassady's lunch hour. Apparently there was a park nearby with a picnic table where they could chat.

Pauling's phone buzzed and she saw the response.

Coming now.

She got out of the car, locked it, and headed toward the entrance of the supply company. She was near the front door when it opened and a fresh-faced young woman with light brown hair, blue eyes and a mask of intense stress stepped out.

Pauling immediately knew it was Cassady.

The woman turned and barely glanced at Pauling as she hurried down the sidewalk, her shoulders hunched forward like she was expecting a raincloud to open up and dump a torrential downpour at any minute.

But the sky was blue.

Not a cloud to be seen.

Pauling turned as well and walked on the opposite side of the street until Cassady turned onto a side street and eventually arrived at the small park she'd mentioned. There was a stand of trees isolating the park from the busy nearby road. A small play structure. A walking path. A family of squirrels scampering around the base of a tree.

The need for subterfuge seemed a little overboard to Pauling, but the fear and anxiety on the woman's face was very real.

Pauling watched Cassady Simmons choose a picnic table on the far side of the park, where she could sit and see the entrance. A little light blue lunch bag was in the woman's hand and she set it on the picnic table.

Good place for a weapon, Pauling thought as she carefully approached.

She slid onto the bench seat across from Cassady.

"Cassady," Pauling said. More of a statement than a question.

The woman closed her eyes. Nodded.

"Tell me what's wrong," Pauling said.

Cassady opened her baby blues and for the first time, the fear dissipated for just a moment.

"I'm surprised I've lived long enough to meet you," she said.

"Now that you see me face-to-face, why don't we start at the beginning?" Pauling asked.

She had her notebook, pen, and cell phone in front of her.

Cassady glanced around, as if someone might be standing nearby with a hyperbolic microphone.

"There's no one here," Pauling assured her. "Just you and me."

Cassady dipped her head as if she was about to literally plunge forward. A long, shaky, breath and then, "It's my husband," she said.

"Rick."

"How did you know?"

"Public records," Pauling said. "I did a little homework."

"Okay, I guess," Cassady said. "He said he thought he was being followed. He got more and more paranoid and then one day, he just didn't come home."

"Come home from where?"

"From work."

"Did you go to the police?"

"No."

"Why not?"

"Because Rick told me not to."

Pauling knitted her brow. "He told you not to? When? Before he disappeared?"

Cassady nodded. "He said that if he ever didn't contact me for awhile, that I shouldn't worry. And he said the police wouldn't be able to help."

"What does he do?"

"He's a truck driver."

Pauling started writing.

"For who?"

"It's called Rio Grande Trucking."

"Did he say who he thought was following him?"

"No."

"Did anyone you know of want to hurt him? Did he have enemies?"

"No. He's an easy going guy," Cassady said. "He hates trouble. It was hard to make him mad, even when we were fighting."

Pauling was tempted to ask how often they fought, but she decided to hold off on that one for now.

"How are your finances? Any money trouble?" Pauling knew more often than not, money was the root of the crime. Or, the lack of money, more accurately.

"Fine," Cassady said. "We're fairly frugal."

"What about drugs and alcohol? Any problems there?"

"Rick likes to drink beer on the weekends, but that's about it. I like white wine. Maybe a mojito when I'm getting crazy," she said. This time, she laughed a little bit and Pauling felt a swell of compassion.

Despite that, she had to ask the next question. "I just have to ask this, I'm sure the answer is no, but was there any infidelity on either side? I don't care one way or the other, I just have to know if I'm going to look into this for you."

"I can't pay you," Cassady said, quickly.

"I understand," Pauling replied.

"And no, no infidelity. That would be–"

She stopped herself, but Pauling instantly intuited what she was going to say. Maybe it was the way Cassady had caught herself, or the insinuation.

"Oh," she said.

Cassady looked at her. "Oh, what?"

"You're pregnant, aren't you?" Pauling asked.

Cassady burst into tears.

19

In the desert, nothing goes to waste. Every drop of water. Every ounce of protein. Every opportunity to obtain sustenance is utilized.

So when the coyote smelled something in the air, its instincts immediately kicked in. She was hungry, and the smell was familiar.

Blood.

Where there was the smell of blood, usually, there was meat.

It took the coyote the better part of ten minutes to triangulate the location of the scent and there, she found the first drop of blood.

One drop led to the next.

And the next.

Soon, there were multiple scent markers telling the coyote a meal was most likely close at hand.

It was a trail for the coyote.

It led her to a clear disturbance in the sand.

An alarm rose within the coyote. This was the smell of something foreign. Something to be feared.

It was the same kind of scent she had discovered around places where bad things happened.

But mixed in with the sense of danger was a delicious smell.

Food.

Life.

The coyote lifted her head and peered into the darkness around her.

She saw no threats. She backed off from the discovery, circled, and then came back.

Nothing had threatened her.

Nothing had leapt out from the darkness to attack.

For the moment, she felt safe enough to investigate further.

She planted a front paw at the edge of the disturbance in the sand.

And then she began to dig.

20

Luckily, probably because she had been crying so often lately, Cassady had a tissue in her purse. She used it to catch the tears before they completely ruined her makeup.

"I really have to get back to the office," she said.

Pauling checked the time and made a decision.

"Do you trust me now?" she asked. "Enough to have a longer conversation?"

Cassady nodded, still wiping her eyes.

"Okay, since you have to get back to work and don't want to look like you had the worst lunch of your life, why don't we continue this conversation at your home?" Pauling asked. "I want to see the house, and maybe we can talk more and start to get some insights into what may have happened."

"Okay," Cassady said. She gave Pauling her address, and Pauling didn't bother to tell her she already had it. It would just freak the girl out even more.

They walked back together and parted in front of the door Cassady had emerged from earlier.

"I still don't understand something, though," Cassady said. "If you're not involved in whatever happened to Rick, how did you get involved? I mean, I didn't contact you. So who did?"

"That's part of why I'm here," Pauling said. "I don't know the answer to that, either. But the way I'm looking at it, once I have my answer, you'll probably have yours, too."

Cassady nodded and Pauling put a hand on her shoulder.

"We'll figure this thing out together, okay?" she said.

Cassady gave a half-hearted smile and walked through the door back into her building.

Pauling's words of encouragement had sounded even hollow to her. The truth was, she had no idea how she was going to get to the bottom of Rick Simmons' disappearance. Already, she was having doubts about Cassady's ability to help and figured the meeting tonight with her would probably produce very little.

Still, she had to remain positive.

And most of all, she wanted to find out Jack Reacher's involvement.

Pauling went back to her Impala, put the car in gear and drove away.

She would check into a hotel, hook up her laptop, do some more research and then head out to meet Cassady.

There was something about the girl and the situation that just didn't add up. Pauling felt like she was missing something, something obvious but she couldn't force it to crystallize. It was like a memory you just couldn't place.

Pauling headed into downtown Albuquerque.

She felt like staying in a nice hotel with a gym.

Maybe she had just enough time to work out some of the kinks from the flight.

21

The plane was being flown by a sixty-year-old man who'd left the advertising business to pursue his passion for aviation. Often times, in long meetings at the agency, he would daydream about being in his little plane, taking to the skies, flying over and above everything. A quiet and peaceful world where he was in control.

His office had sported all things aviation. An airplane clock. A paper clip holder in the shape of a fuselage. A coffee table featuring landing gear for supports.

Eventually, he'd saved enough money to lease a little hangar and keep his pride and joy, a Piper Cherokee from the 1970s, in excellent flying condition. He planned to fly as long as he possibly could. He was only sixty years old, and his savvy investing had paid off with a retirement fund that kicked off more than enough to keep what was normally a fairly expensive hobby from draining him dry.

Now, he'd spent a good amount of the afternoon crisscrossing the desert and the mountains, doing a big loop and enjoying near-perfect weather.

He never felt more at peace than he did in the air.

It seemed to put all of the world's issues into perspective. Made them seem smaller somehow.

Now, he was on his way back to the airstrip just outside of Albuquerque. He would land, stow the plane, maybe hang out in his little hangar for an hour or two, nursing a whiskey and replaying the flight in his mind.

But his reverie was interrupted when he spotted something in the desert below.

With casual ease, he maneuvered the plane around for a closer look, dropping in altitude as he made his run.

The ground flew past him in a blur, but ahead, he saw a shape on the ground.

As his plane sped forward, the image came closer and closer until he was able to confirm what he thought he'd seen.

A body.

There was a definite shape of a torso, along with some limbs.

A pack of coyotes scattered as he flew overhead.

There was no doubt in his mind as he prepared to call in what he'd seen.

It had been a body.

Or at least, what was left of it.

22

Pauling chose an upscale hotel that belonged to a family of luxury properties, mainly because she knew they would have some of the amenities most important to her.

Room service coffee, twenty-four hours a day. A gym. And reliable Internet service.

She checked in, didn't bother unpacking, plugged in her laptop and put on workout clothes. She headed down to the fitness center, was pleasantly surprised by its extensive collection of machines and free weights, and put in forty-five minutes of intense exertion.

Afterward, she showered, dressed and checked the time.

She had an hour to kill before she had to rendezvous with Cassady. Pauling decided to use the time to plow through her always-accruing email.

There were status updates from subcontractors on other active cases. Initial queries on new investigations. Purchase order requests. And then there was yet another email from a huge competitor who wanted to buy Pauling's company, along with her services.

They were pursuing her mostly because they kept losing business to her.

If you can't beat 'em, buy 'em. That was their strategy. It had worked for a lot of holding companies, Pauling knew.

They also wanted her because of her pedigree. They were apparently having a hard time matching it, when it came to selling themselves to new clients.

Pauling politely declined their offer.

The money was certainly attention-getting, however. She could sell her private investigative company, buy a villa in the south of France...and what? Sit on the beach all day? Go through a bunch of lovers on vacation? Develop a drinking problem?

The fact was, her job was important to her. She had family, sure. A sister in Portland with three children.

It was good to visit them. Pauling even looked forward to seeing everybody.

They were as close as two sisters could be who'd chosen distinctly different life paths.

Pauling could still have kids, through adoption. Maybe one day she would. She certainly had the financial resources to give a child everything they could need.

But her job demanded travel.

And the ability to drop everything on a moment's notice and just go. The last time she'd checked, that wasn't a good lifestyle for a single mother.

That spontaneity was essential to the life of a private investigator.

Just like this case.

The Reacher File.

That's how she thought of it. She didn't consider it the Cassady Simmons Case.

It was the Reacher File.

Pauling had taken the mystery letter with the phone number, put it in a folder, and filed it under the name "Reacher."

Perhaps she'd done it because she felt wistful thinking of Jack Reacher.

Or, perhaps it just made sense.

Checking the clock on her laptop, Pauling saw it was time to go.

She snapped her laptop shut. Put on her holster and slipped her gun into its spot. She double-checked her keys and phone and then left the room. She put the Do Not Disturb sign on the door handle.

Pauling retrieved the Impala, pulled out of the hotel parking garage and pointed the big vehicle toward the home of Cassady Simmons.

She would be there in fifteen minutes.

23

Petrie was summoned to Rollins' office. It was a corner space, with a window on each side. The view wasn't much, just the side of another building, but at least natural light made its way in.

Which seemed misplaced. In contrast to the content of the discussion.

"How good is Hess?" Rollins asked.

"She's good. Sharp. Ivy League. Not afraid to do what has to be done."

Rollins was sitting in his chair, his cell phone on the desk in front of him. Petrie remained standing.

"Have you read the safeguards that were in

place to prevent this exact kind of thing from happening?"

"I have."

"And?"

Petrie sighed. "Nearly all preventive measures in this type of situation are to minimize the impact of human error."

"This wasn't error."

"The side product of this approach is that it also eliminates windows of opportunity for folks with bad intentions. The more processes that are automated and regulated, remove bad actors from the equation."

"A good theory."

"The one drawback nearly every operation of this type has is that the human element can never be fully removed," Petrie said. "Otherwise it becomes Artificial Intelligence. Which has its own worst-case scenarios."

"Indeed," Rollins asserted.

"Suffice to say, this was a combination of human interaction combined with technologic savvy."

"Had to be," Rollins agreed.

"So unless you are willing to take human

beings completely out of the equation, you will always be dancing with the devil."

Rollins raised an eyebrow at Petrie.

"Dancing with the devil?"

"It's all about odds. You limit the number of people with access to certain things, but you always have to have someone there. And no matter how much you lower the odds, mathematically, there's always the potential for the dice to land on the wrong spot."

"And now we're adding someone else to the equation," Rollins said. "I hope Hess can handle this."

"She's not alone, sir," Petrie pointed out. "I'm monitoring this thing from start to finish. And like I said, Ostertag is capable. He and his team can accomplish whatever Hess asks them to do. If need be, we can provide more support to Hess once she makes an initial assessment."

Rollins swiped his cell phone from his desk and looked at the screen.

"Okay. Let's get this thing taken care of. No more surprises."

Petrie was about to answer, but Rollins had put the phone to his ear.

He let himself out of the office.

24

Pauling turned down the street that Cassady Simmons called home, and began looking for the correct house number.

It was a modest neighborhood, full of single-story homes, many with Spanish tile roofs and white stucco. Some had garages, most didn't. Cars were parked in driveways and landscapes featured mostly rock and thin shrubbery, punctuated by the occasional cactus plant. Walkways were paved with dark red stones, often bordered with white edging.

Ahead, she saw a full-sized sedan parked along the curb. Something about it gave Pauling pause.

It looked like a cop car.

Or a Bureau car.

And it appeared to be parked in front of the house bearing Cassady's address.

Pauling parked behind the car, noted its license plate number and exited the Impala. She walked to the front door. Before ringing the bell, she listened. There was no sound. Pauling turned around and looked back at the car.

Okay, decision time.

One, it could be that the owners of the mystery car weren't here, at Cassady's house. Maybe they were visiting the home across the street. Two, maybe Cassady herself wasn't even home yet. Three, if Cassady was home, and there was someone inside with her, would ringing the bell make sense?

Pauling weighed her options.

Suddenly, it occurred to her that maybe she had slightly discounted Cassady's fear. Had the young woman finally called the police? Had she ignored her husband's advice not to call them? Had they sent out a pair of detectives?

At times like this, Pauling trusted her instincts. And right now, they told her to test the door first and see if it was unlocked. She reached forward, and turned the doorknob. The latch clicked open.

Unlocked.

Now she knew.

There was no way Cassady Simmons in her current state of mind would leave the front door unlocked.

Pauling gently pushed the door open and stepped inside the house.

Staring back at her, with a disappointed look on his face, was a man with a gun.

25

Michael Tallon's behavior wasn't governed by money. Most of what he'd done professionally in his life had been because he believed in something. His father had been a bit of a genius with numbers and had found a home in the accounting industry. His son had shared some of the ability, but none of the desire.

He had been captivated at an early age by a belief in his country. It was something he'd come to organically, and it had blossomed within him as a young man.

It was why he'd chosen to enter the military.

Still, money was money.

You had to respect it.

Or it would make you pay.

Tallon kept close tabs on his modest invest-ment portfolio, and particularly focused moni-toring of his liquid investments. It was something his father had taught him.

He had done well in his career so far and through various efforts, had achieved a steady income from both his military and government work. He had invested shrewdly and his return was steady. Some now might even say he was fairly well off.

But Tallon lived for something more.

So, he logged out of his banking and invest-ment accounts, went to the kitchen and grabbed a beer.

His casita featured an open kitchen, with clean lines and high-end finishes. Tallon had sprung to have a professional designer do his space, with certain adaptions that he needed for his line of work.

A sliding glass door opened out onto a rear deck, with a stone fire pit in the middle. Tallon loved to sit out here when the evening cooled down, with a small fire, a beer in hand, looking out at the distant mountains.

He sat in a chair, and put his feet up on the

edge of the fire pit, contemplated building a fire. He used juniper wood and the scent was oddly comforting to him.

He drank his beer and thought about his run in the desert.

How something had troubled him.

It was still there, in the back of his mind.

The sense that something was about to happen.

When it did, he knew he would be ready.

And as always, he hoped he would be given the opportunity to do something good. Maybe even, to right a wrong.

26

Threw man with the gun didn't hesitate.

And neither did Pauling.

As he raised his gun to fire, she dove left, into a space off the hallway that turned out to be a living room.

Something exploded behind her and Pauling knew that the front door had received the round meant for her. She heard plaster explode and chunks of it landed on the floor.

Pauling got to her feet with her gun in hand as the sound of gunshots continued to echo in the hallway.

Well, the car outside didn't belong to cops, she knew that now. And she felt a sudden surge of anger, not just at the shooter in the hall, but at herself. Cassady had been right to fear for her life. Pauling felt awful that she had simply sent the woman back to work.

Now, Pauling scooted close to the edge of the wall and took a quick peek around into the hallway.

The man was gone.

Pauling darted back into the living room and looked to the other end of the space. There was a pass-through to the kitchen and an opening to the right of the room that no doubt doubled back to the hallway.

That's where the man with the gun would be if he planned to ambush her again. Or, it would be the way he would come for her.

It was the obvious choice.

Maybe he was hoping she would stay looking toward the hallway which would mean he'd have a clear chance to shoot her in the back.

Well, that wasn't going to happen.

Pauling ducked down and crossed the living area to the edge of the pass-through. She took a quick look.

It was a narrow kitchen, with an opening on the other side into a dining room. It was a basic setup. Stove. Refrigerator. A little bit of counter space and some cabinets. A small table with two chairs.

No sign of the shooter.

Pauling kept moving, crossed the pass-through into the kitchen with her gun extended in front of her.

The kitchen was empty and so was the hallway.

Pauling ducked into the dining room. Empty.

She could see through the kitchen into the living room but there was no one there.

Which left the hallway and the rooms beyond.

Suddenly, at the rear of the house, Pauling heard a thump and then a door slammed.

She carefully moved forward, using the edge of the wall for protection. She darted through the hallway into an open door across from the kitchen and in her peripheral vision, she saw the man with the gun at the end of the hallway.

His pistol was raised and he shot, but Pauling had already flung herself forward. Chunks of plaster from the wall behind her flew in all directions.

Pauling wheeled around and was about to fire.

But the man was gone.

The door at the end of the hallway was wide open.

She moved quickly forward.

It was a small house. The first room on the right was a bathroom.

It was empty.

Pauling leaned against the bathroom's door-jamb. Outside, she heard a car start up, followed by the sound of squealing tires and an engine racing.

Pauling ducked back into the hallway, moved quickly down the hall to the door on the right. She took a quick look inside.

It was a bedroom with a dresser, two windows, and a body on the floor.

It was Cassady.

She wasn't moving.

27

The car emblazoned with the logo of the New Mexico State Police pulled off the highway and its driver looked into the distance.

His name was Paul Veasy and he'd gotten the call that an aircraft had notified dispatch a body had been seen out in the desert.

Not exactly big news in this area. The desert was a harsh and unrelenting place. Homeless people. Drug addicts. Folks suffering from mental illness. When they went into the desert they usually didn't come back.

Now, Veasy looked at the sun in the sky, and mentally ran through the past few days, weather-wise. It had been hot with very little cloud cover.

Great for the golfers, not so good for a person lost and perhaps in a weakened state.

The pilot had been fastidious with pinpointing its location, and Veasy had gotten the call.

Veasy debated about driving his vehicle into the desert, but decided against it. One, even though the terrain was obviously flat, there were occasional boulders, well camouflaged to completely blend into the landscape. More than one trooper had managed to rip out pieces of his squad car's underpinnings by being too aggressive in taking his vehicle off-road. In cop shows on television, a character's penchant for ruining squad cars was often a lighthearted joke. Not so in the real world. Your car was your responsibility. You could get a black mark in your employee file if you were careless with it.

Two, Veasy was on a diet. He'd joined Weight Watchers, was now down fifteen pounds, and was constantly looking for reasons to exercise. On the program, food was correlated to a point system and the more he exercised, the more points he earned. The more points he earned, the more food he could eat. And Paul Veasy loved food. It was how he'd ended up in Weight Watchers in the first place.

So, Trooper Veasy shut off his vehicle, pocketed the keys, locked her up and walked toward a patch of land currently being overseen by two vultures circling overhead.

It took him about fifteen minutes to reach the corpse.

It had been torn apart, but Veasy could see it was a man. The work boots, jeans and shirt all told him the deceased was male. What was left of the face and other areas of exposed skin were all charred black.

Ethnicity was impossible to estimate.

Veasy carefully stepped around the body, and slipped a hand into the front pockets. They were empty.

He gently lifted the body and found a wallet.

He opened it and studied its contents.

There was a New Mexico driver's license.

With a photo and a name.

Rick Simmons.

28

P auling went to Cassady, pivoted so she was facing the doorway and couldn't be ambushed, and knelt down next to her. She saw the duct tape around the woman's wrists, and quickly turned her so she could see her face. Cassady's wide eyes stared out at her in terror, another strip of duct tape was across her mouth.

Pauling held up her finger to indicate she needed a second. She then left the room, checked the bedroom across the hall, and raced to the front of the house.

The mystery car was gone.

Pauling grabbed a small paring knife from the kitchen, went back to Cassady, and cut her hands free.

"This is going to hurt a little bit," Pauling said, and then pulled the tape from Cassady's mouth.

"Owwwww," Cassady said, and then burst into tears.

Pauling helped her to her feet, and guided her toward the kitchen.

"We need to call the police," Pauling said, and reached for her cell phone.

"No!" Cassady barked at her. "No. They have Rick."

"Did they say that?"

"No."

"Then how do you know?"

"Why else would they be here trying to get me, too?"

Pauling wasn't sure she could answer that. She hadn't gotten a very good look at the man who'd shot at her. He'd been a white guy, in jeans and a dark jacket. Black shoes.

"Why don't you tell me what happened?"

Cassady sat in one of the chairs at the kitchen table and Pauling got her a glass of water, then sat across from her.

"That's just it, I don't know what happened," Cassady said. She took a drink of water and then gulped the rest.

"Why don't you start with when you came home from work?"

Cassady nodded.

Pauling knew that someone had heard the gunshots and the cops would most likely be arriving soon, despite Cassady's desire not to call them.

"I came home from work, changed, and was getting ready for your visit when someone grabbed me from behind. I don't know how they got into the house."

Pauling knew. If they had Rick Simmons, they no doubt had his keys to the house. No need to break in. Just use the key and let yourself in. Easy.

They took me back to my room and I thought they were going to rape me."

"You said 'they.' Why do you think there was more than one person?"

"When I came to I could hear them talking."

"What were they saying?"

"I don't know. I thought I heard them say Rick's name, but I can't be sure."

In the distance, Pauling heard a siren.

"Cassady, I need you to think. Why would someone be after you and Rick? You're absolutely right. If they already have Rick, why do they want you?"

The young woman burst into tears.

"I have no idea," she said.

29

The bald man with the bulging veins was not pleased. He didn't show it to his subordinates, however. Any sign of negative emotion was not helpful. It was its own form of weakness.

He simply remained staring at them.

"It was supposed to be a grab and go," the smaller of the two men said. He was thin and wiry. A relatively new employee. He was also the most nervous of the two. The other one, a tall man, knew better than to speak. He'd been working for the bald man for quite some time.

"How were we supposed to know that some chick would show up? She was some kind of cop, too."

"So you failed to bring Cassady Simmons here," the bald man said.

"Well, yeah. But it wasn't our fault." The shorter man looked at his coworker for support and possible vindication, but he was greeted with silence.

These were excuses, and everyone in the room knew it.

The bald man contemplated the human beings before him. That was one of the intrinsic failures of evolution. It didn't create perfection. People died all the time, mostly because of gaps in the evolutionary process. A lack of knowledge. A momentary lapse of awareness. One had to recognize the fallibility of their own minds and bodies. Too few did.

Hundreds of years ago, a failure to recognize a danger in the environment meant certain death. Genetic material that played any kind of role in that failure, was also eliminated. It couldn't be passed along.

It was the beauty of evolution.

Natural selection.

The two men stood waiting for their superior's response.

He was still contemplating the laws of nature.

In the wild, a human being could wander out into the night, get snatched up by a tiger, and that particular personality trait would become less apparent in the population.

The bald man did not believe in God. He believed in science. In physics. In the power of the natural world.

He understood, however, that at this moment he was a part of that evolutionary process. He could either be the tiger in the night who eliminated the weakness in these two men, or he could allow the undesirable trait to continue. Perhaps the fear they were obviously experiencing right now would curb that predilection.

That might be true.

It also seemed like the best approach was to split the difference.

The bald man pulled the gun from its resting spot in the small of his back, raised it and fired. The bullet struck the short man on the right, and blew off the top of his head.

The body sagged to the ground.

The tall man hadn't moved, despite blood spray flecking his face.

Although he didn't show it, he felt vindicated

by his decision not to speak. Unless his boss was going to shoot him, too, it had been a life-and-death decision.

Instead of a bullet, he received an order.

"Throw him in the incinerator."

30

"Let's try to work this out," Pauling said.

She had finally gotten Cassady under control. The tears had stopped, but the young woman was still shaking. Pauling had poured her a glass of water from the kitchen counter, and let her drink while she performed some security.

Pauling went to the doors and windows and made sure everything was locked. She dead bolted the door.

While she went through the house, she studied the belongings. It was all to be expected. Basic furniture, probably from one of the big warehouse furniture stores. Nothing very expensive. Nothing unique.

There were a few framed prints of desert flowers on the walls, and the rest were pictures of Cassady and Rick. Some of their parents and extended family as well.

It looked like the home of a relatively young couple about to start a family.

Pauling made her way back to Cassady.

"What am I supposed to do?" the young woman asked her. Her voice was more steady, but still a little shaky. She looked like someone whose world had been turned upside down, more than once.

There was no doubt how awful Cassady must feel, Pauling thought. Her husband's missing, no family nearby, her home invaded, attacked, and now the only person here to help is someone she just met. Someone who Cassady doesn't even really know.

Pauling decided the wrong way to go about this was to start telling Cassady what to do. For starters, she didn't even know where to begin. And to start listing things for the young woman to do would only overwhelm her more.

So she decided to take a different approach, and get Cassady's mind off of herself.

"Let me tell you a little bit about myself,"

Pauling said. She gave Cassady the rundown on her background, including her work at the FBI with kidnapping and other types of cases. She also told her a little about the Anne Lane case, leaving out the part about Jack Reacher.

"But I still don't know how you found me," Cassady said. "How do I know you're not one of them?"

"Well, for starters, I didn't try to kidnap you," Pauling pointed out. "If I was one of them, I would have helped them get you into their car or something. And they shot at me, I didn't shoot at them."

"Yeah," Cassady said. "Unless you just want to appear to be my friend to get something from me."

"Something like what?" Pauling asked. She wasn't being a smart-ass. The fact was, there was a possibility that Rick Simmons had been taken in an effort to get something. That attempt had failed. So now they were coming to Cassady for whatever it might be.

Pauling didn't think so, but since it had come up, she thought she would pursue it.

"It can't be anything. I would have given them whatever they asked for to get Rick back. But we don't have anything," she said, her voice on the verge of breaking into sobs again. "We have, like, five hundred dollars in our checking account."

"Right," Pauling said. "So if you don't have anything, what could I possibly be after?"

"That's true," Cassady admitted.

"Also, I wanted to go to the police. You didn't. If I were doing something illegal or trying to harm you, I highly doubt I would have suggested the cops."

"I'm sorry, I do trust you," Cassady said. "I'm just scared. And sick of this shit. And I miss Rick."

She started crying again.

Pauling was about to say something when the doorbell rang. She got up, walked to the living room, with her hand on her gun.

What the hell was it now, she thought.

Pauling looked out toward the front and saw exactly what she had hoped she wouldn't.

Two police cars.

31

"Cassady Simmons?"

The cop peering in at Pauling was young, with big brown eyes, a hawk nose, and thick black hair swept straight back. There was another man in back, an older cop. They both looked solemn.

Pauling immediately knew what that meant.

Oh no.

She hesitated before answering the cops, but there was no other way. There wasn't time to soften the blow she knew with certainty was coming.

"Sure, let me get her. Come in," she said.

Pauling walked back to the kitchen and Cassady looked up at her. It was a horrible moment for Pauling, because she knew what was about to happen and felt incredibly guilty that Cassady didn't. There was no way to prepare her, though.

"The police are here," Pauling said.

"I said not to call them!" Cassady hissed at her. A mixture of terror and anger swirled behind Cassady's big blue eyes. Her mouth was set in a tight, grim line.

"I didn't call them," Pauling said.

"Well who did?"

"Someone probably heard the gunshots. Or maybe nobody called them and they're here for a different reason," Pauling said, trying to prepare Cassady for what was most likely to transpire.

Cassady's eyes went wide and she jumped up from her chair and practically ran down the hallway to the police.

Pauling trailed her, heard the cops break the news.

Cassady let out a long wail, a painful scream, and collapsed.

The two cops caught her in their arms.

Pauling pointed to the couch in the living room.

They carried the young woman to the couch and Pauling grabbed a pillow, to rest Cassady's head. There was a throw blanket on one of the chairs. Pauling put that over Cassady.

She turned to the older cop and gestured for him to follow her into the hallway.

"Tell me what you found," Pauling said.

The old cop looked at her with bemused skepticism.

"And exactly who are you?"

"Lauren Pauling."

"Okay, Lauren Pauling. Now tell me who you are and why you're here. Family? Friend?"

"A friend."

The cop had taken out a notebook and pen, ready to take notes.

"Do you know her husband? Rick Simmons?"

"Never met him," Pauling said. "I'm a friend of Cassady. She called me because she was worried about Rick. Do you know anything about that?"

The old cop tapped his pen against the notepad, weighed his options.

"You have some ID?" the cop asked.

Pauling showed him her driver's license.

"New York, huh?"

"So what's the deal with Rick?" Pauling asked, ignoring his question.

Finally, he glanced toward the living room and

then back at Pauling. "Rick was found deceased in the desert." His voice was low, but Pauling could tell he'd done this before. Probably many times.

Pauling just nodded. She had figured that was the reason for the police stopping by, and from their body language. Breaking this kind of news never put a bounce in anyone's step.

"Cause of death?" she asked.

The older cop looked at her. He had a weathered face, deeply lined and tan. His eyes were blue, and accepted no bullshit.

"Are you sure you're just a friend of the family?" he asked.

"Friend. And private investigator," Pauling said. "We can talk about that later, though. Cause of death?"

He shook his head. "Not for public consumption. Were you a cop? You seem like it."

"FBI," Pauling said. "Formerly."

The old cop gave a little smirk. "Figures."

He brushed past her and walked toward the living room. Pauling followed him and watched as he joined his young partner standing next to Cassady, who was now curled up on the couch. In the fetal position, numb with shock. Her worst nightmare had come true.

Pauling knew what was going to happen next. They would want to bring Cassady to the station to identify the body. They would probably put her in an interview room afterward and ask her a ton of questions. Pauling was confident Cassady had nothing to hide, but she still thought about finding the young woman an attorney. She filed the thought away for the moment.

Instead, it was Pauling's intention to take Cassady to the police station. The poor woman had no one now. Maybe there was extended family, but in the meantime, Pauling was it.

She really wanted someone to go out to the crime scene. She wanted to find out where the body had been found and look at it before nature ran its course. She was licking her investigative chops but couldn't do anything, as she had to protect Cassady from further harm.

Pauling ran through the people with whom she had worked previously in the area. Immediately, one named jumped out way ahead of the rest.

They had worked together several times, once when she was still with the Bureau.

Pauling almost smiled at herself.

It would be good to see Michael Tallon again.

32

Tallon looked at his phone. A call was coming in and the number was linked to a contact in his phone's database.

Lauren Pauling.

A small smirk tugged at the corner of his mouth.

Now there was a woman, he thought. He pictured her in his mind. Really quite beautiful, with golden hair, a killer body and gorgeous eyes. A little older than him, she had a timeless look about her. Not to mention that she could pass for a woman probably ten maybe even fifteen years younger.

But it was that voice.

The voice is what he remembered.

A little raspy. Like a blues singer just before her first cup of coffee in the morning.

He slid his thumb along the phone's screen to answer the call.

"Pauling," he said.

"Are you out in the middle of the desert?" she asked him. "Running for your life with vultures circling overhead?"

They had worked together a few times previously, both in official capacities with the government, and later, when they both went into private contract work.

Pauling had even been to his house and witnessed his intense physical regimen firsthand. It had been all business, though, despite his best efforts.

"Nope. Middle of the garage," he said.

It was true, he had fashioned a home gym in the garage and was in the middle of lifting. There was a window, but he kept it shut. He liked the heat and the sweat. As the saying went, the only easy day was yesterday.

"Squats or bench press?" she asked him.

"Deadlifts."

There was a pause, and then Pauling said, "So you're not on a job at the moment, I can assume?"

"You assume correctly," Tallon answered. He sat down on the end of the weight bench. A puddle of sweat was forming beneath him and he snatched a towel from one of the barbells, used it to wipe his face so he wouldn't smear it all over his phone.

"How about you join me in Albuquerque?" Pauling asked.

"Albuquerque?" Tallon asked. "What the hell's in Albuquerque?"

"That's what I'm trying to figure out," Pauling answered. "I need someone who can do some investigating, as well as possibly performing asset protection. The situation is rather fluid at the moment."

Tallon ran through the calendar in his head. He had a job tentatively on the books for next month, but nothing at the moment. He'd planned to catch up on paperwork and put in extra time in the desert as well as on the gun range.

Well, that could wait.

"When do you need me there?" he asked. They would figure out the financial aspects later. Tallon knew that Pauling would pay him fairly.

"Yesterday," she said.

Tallon ran through what he needed to do

before he could leave, and his best guess at the length of the trip. "I can be there in about eight hours," he said. "I'm going to drive so I don't have to deal with airport restrictions." Meaning, he planned to bring more firepower than certain regulations allowed.

"Good. I'll text you the address," she said.

"Looking forward to it," he said, and he had a small smile on his face. He was looking forward to seeing her again. And hearing that voice.

He didn't expect a response and when she disconnected, he wasn't surprised. Pauling was smart and tough. She didn't have time to play games and neither did Tallon.

The thought of time prompted him to check his watch.

It would take him fifteen minutes to finish his workout and then he would start to assemble his gear. His vehicle already had a full tank of gas and he kept everything neat and tidy. It was his way of always being ready to leave at a moment's notice.

The workout, however, was not something he would cut short.

Tallon always finished what he started.

33

Special Agent Jacqueline Hess arrived in Albuquerque.

The flight had been efficient and relatively painless. She'd spent the majority of her time reviewing all of the files and documents Petrie had given her on her way out the door.

It had been a lot.

But Hess was a fast reader and a quick learner. Data was power. Her mind was a model of efficiency and precision. She was born to be an analyst and she knew it.

Hess also knew that her beliefs and convictions were just as powerful as the best kind of analysis.

The moment the plane's wheels touched ground, her phone lit up.

There were messages from Petrie, back at headquarters, as well as from the head of the Albuquerque office, SAC Ray Ostertag.

Hess breezed through the messages from head-quarters as they were mostly request for status updates. This always amused her when requests for updates were placed with no attention paid to time. Did Petrie want an update on how the flight went? Hardly.

The message she focused on was from Ostertag and it told her that a car was waiting for her outside of baggage claim.

Hess used the restroom, retrieved her gear, grabbed a coffee to go and stepped out into the warm, dry air of New Mexico.

She recognized the power of the moment. That first breath of fresh air, not stale and recycled like in the airplane and the airport itself. This was real. She was here, and Hess couldn't shake the fact that it felt like all of her life had been leading up to this point. There was a lot riding on this.

Like her entire future.

Well, she couldn't let it get to her. She had to perform. And perform well. So she shook off any jitters and focused on the task at hand.

Hess spotted her ride immediately. A Crown

Vic, charcoal gray, with light gray interior. Direct from the FBI car pool, she was sure.

A young agent in a white shirt, dark jacket and tie, sat behind the wheel. He glanced over and nodded at her, then got out and popped the trunk.

"Agent Hess," he said. "I'm McIlroy."

She shook his hand and then slid into the front passenger seat.

They didn't speak as McIlroy put the car into gear and pointed it toward downtown.

"We should be there in ten minutes or so," McIlroy said.

Hess ignored him and watched the scenery change from airport industrial to desert with a freeway running through it.

She wondered how long she would be stuck in Albuquerque.

For some reason, her guess was that it would be longer than the good folks back at headquarters were assuming.

34

The good news for Cassady was that identifying the body was not necessary. Pauling knew it was probably because of the condition of the corpse and it would have to be accomplished through dental records.

The bad news was, she was indeed questioned at the police station by the two detectives who had arrived at the house.

During the process, Cassady was barely holding it together. Although because Pauling wasn't allowed into the interview room, she had no real idea of how it went.

As Pauling waited, she saw a man enter the squad room, and make his way over to the interview room where Cassady was being questioned.

He was an older man, with a dark suit and a crewcut.

Pauling recognized the FBI when she saw it.

Why was the FBI involved? Pauling thought.

The questioning continued until eventually the older cop brought Cassady out. No one else came out of the interview room.

"What's with the Feebie?" Pauling asked.

The cop ignored her.

"We'll touch base with you if we have any more questions, Cassady," he said. "In the meantime, do you need a ride home? Or will Ms. Pauling here be taking you?"

"I've got it," Pauling said.

She steered Cassady out of the squad room, out of the building and into her rental car.

Pauling knew better than to ask Cassady what they had discussed. Pauling knew exactly what kind of questions they would have trotted out. However, she was extremely interested in the FBI man.

But Cassady was in no shape to answer any more questions.

They would simply have to wait.

Pauling felt a deep compassion for the young woman who had left the police with nothing at all.

Since Rick's death was ruled a homicide, all evidence collected was kept with the cops. She had nothing from her husband now, but memories.

Pauling took her back to her house, and found some Benadryl in the medicine chest. It would have been better to have a Valium, but not for a pregnant woman.

Cassady went to bed, exhausted, and on the verge of both a physical and mental collapse. Pauling had told her she was bringing in some extra security for her until things settled down. She wasn't sure Cassady even heard her as she was in a total and complete fog.

Pauling buttoned up the security of the house and got a text message.

She glanced at her phone.

Tallon was pulling up in the driveway.

Pauling went to the front door, glanced out from a side window as she never trusted peepholes.

It was too easy for a perp to stand at a front door, put his gun to the peephole, and wait for the light beneath the door to change slightly. Pull the trigger, shoot the person on the other side of the door through the eye.

It had happened before.

This time, however, instead of an assassin waiting to fire a round, Pauling saw Tallon watching her from the front step.

He was looking over at the side window with a smile on his face.

It gave her a moment of relief from the drama of the day to see him.

She smiled, in spite of herself, and opened the door.

"I don't trust peepholes, either," he said.

35

"Heads are going to roll for this one," Rollins said.

He had just walked into Petrie's office, a much smaller, much less impressive space than his own.

Petrie was at his desk, reading through a status report he'd already reviewed twice. There was no new information, but sometimes a second and even a third look bring something new to the surface.

Not this time.

He watched Rollins sink into a chair across from him.

"Anything?" Rollins asked.

Petrie stifled the urge to frown. Hess had just

gotten to Albuquerque and was en route to meet with Ostertag. What could she possibly have accomplished this soon?

"We'll know more when Hess files her first update," Petrie said, his voice cautious. He had carefully phrased his response to include the words 'know more' when the truth was they didn't know anything just yet.

Other than what had already transpired.

Petrie was also struggling to make out the nuances of his boss's expression. That phrase about heads were going to roll could be taken many ways. It all depended on the expression. A threat? An urge to cooperate? Stating the obvious? Most importantly, exactly *whose* heads were going to roll?

Petrie resisted the urge to rub his neck.

"We can still get ahead of this thing," Petrie said. It was something he sort of believed, but it sounded like the perfect thing to say. The truth was, he had no idea if there was time to be proactive.

Rollins rocked back in his chair. He put his feet up on his desk and Petrie absentmindedly noted the brand. Cole Haan.

"Worst-case scenario?" Rollins asked.

Petrie contemplated the question.

"About as bad as it could possibly get. For everyone involved."

Meaning, not just the actual people responsible. But even those with indirect responsibility would pay the price.

"How do you see the worst-case scenario playing out?" Rollins persisted.

Petrie sighed. "It depends what you mean. Are we talking total numbers? Areas affected? The usual political fallout and blame game?"

Rollins grimaced.

"Even in general terms it's horrible," he said. "I imagine the specifics would be even worse."

"They are," Petrie said.

"Let's start with the area affected. What are your thoughts?"

"Let's start with the most difficult."

"That would be when. We have no idea of a timetable, or even if there is one. There has been no communication. No ultimatums. Nothing."

"Okay, so we don't know when. What about where? Best guesses?"

Petrie let out a long, slow whistle.

"Huge. A huge area." Petrie said.

"I know. But which huge area. There's gotta be some indication."

"It would be a guess. Based on nothing other than proximity, access and value of target. And it's my guess, not the team's. We've still got a lot of data to collect."

Rollins raised an eyebrow, waiting for Petrie's answer.

"Los Angeles."

36

"Have you ever met Jack Reacher?" Pauling asked. She had filled Tallon in on what had happened back in New York, starting with the mystery letter emblazoned with Jack Reacher's name.

Cassady was resting in the other room and Pauling had taken Tallon out to the back patio to talk privately. Even though the young woman was asleep, Pauling wanted to make sure their conversation couldn't be overheard.

It was a warm night, with stars scattered across the night sky. The house wasn't too far from a busy street, and they could occasionally hear the sound of traffic, a horn honking in anger or warning.

Pauling couldn't remember if Tallon had ever

come across Reacher in his time in the military, or in some of the investigative cases he'd taken on since he'd left. Their world, ex-military working as civilian investigators, was a small one. Technically, Reacher wasn't an investigator, Pauling knew. His cases were simply instances of Reacher walking into something...and someone...who needed help.

"No, never met Jack Reacher," Tallon said. "I've heard a few stories, though," he said.

"Good stories or bad?"

"Good, mostly. But they aren't really stories. More like rumors along the grapevine, you know. One guy heard from another guy about this thing that happened," Tallon said. "You know how it goes. Military guys are a bunch of gossips."

Pauling laughed. She enjoyed Michael Tallon's presence. He was smaller than Reacher, but then again, who wasn't? A little over six feet, but solid muscle. He had brown hair, cut short, a strong jaw and light green eyes. More often than not, the eyes contained a trace of humor. But when they turned to flint, she could tell they'd seen more than their fair share of violence.

"I didn't realize you guys were a bunch of gossips," she said. "Maybe I'll have to watch what I say around you."

"Is Reacher really involved in this?" Tallon asked.

"I really have no idea," Pauling said. "In an indirect way, he's the reason I'm out here. Somehow he's involved in this, but I have no idea how or why. However, if his name hadn't been included, I probably wouldn't have come out here."

"He was an MP, right?" Tallon asked? "An investigator?"

Pauling nodded. "Yes. Army. One of the best I've ever seen."

"Does the woman here..."

"Cassady."

"Cassady. Does she know him?"

"No. She says she never heard the name before. And that her husband, Rick, had never mentioned him, either."

"Okay, a mystery on top of a mystery."

"Wrapped in an enigma."

They both sat in silence for a moment.

"So they took her husband," Tallon said. "Killed him. And then they came after her. So why didn't they take them together?"

"Opportunity," Pauling said. "He's a truck driver, right? Rarely home? They had to do it separately. The odds of them being together at an opportune time were probably pretty slim. Better to take one and get the other one later."

"Why the time difference?" Tallon asked. "Why not two separate grab teams? Do them simultaneously? That's what I would do. Have the teams be in constant communication so they can synchronize their movements. No way for one victim to warn the other."

Pauling had thought the same thing herself. They were just brainstorming, though. And it was always good to have someone else to bounce ideas around with.

"Maybe it was a lack of manpower," Pauling said. "Maybe we're dealing with a small crew.

"Could be," Tallon said. "Maybe one main guy and a couple of sidekicks."

"Could be, but I don't think so," Pauling said. "That Crown Vic was new. Well-taken care of. The men were well-dressed. He fired without hesitation. This isn't an amateur operation."

"So what's our plan of attack?" Tallon asked.

"First things first," Pauling said. "You stay here, keep an eye on Cassady. I'm going back to my hotel room, get a few hours rest, and then I'm going to head out to the crime scene. I need to see firsthand where Rick Simmons met his end. And why there."

"Roger that," Tallon said.

Pauling got to her feet.

"Let me know when she's up, and how she's doing. I'll be back mid-morning."

Pauling left, went to her car and headed toward the hotel.

Moments later, a black Crown Vic cruised past the Simmons house, and followed Pauling onto the freeway.

t first light, Pauling was back on the road.

A few hours' sleep.

A good cup of dark roast.

The city was just waking up, the freeway mostly full of truck drivers and road warrior sales people. The occasional tourist family putted along in the slow lane, with the minivan packed, along with a luggage carrier strapped to the top. A hippie couple here or there off to camp in the mountains. Smoke dope and drink coffee, contemplate the universe.

Pauling was contemplating the situation.

Rick Simmons, murdered in the desert.

An attempted abduction of Cassady Simmons.

She decided to start there. Why an abduction? Why kill her husband, and not her? Why kill him, but only kidnap her?

That didn't make sense to Pauling.

Unless they wanted something from the husband, who refused to give it up, and died in the process.

So then they moved on to Cassady.

That was a possibility.

Another angle was that they planned to kill Cassady, too, eventually. The abduction may have only been step one in the process. They'd been interrupted. Maybe the plan had been to kidnap Cassady, take her somewhere, and torture her. Clearly, they were after something. The problem was, Pauling didn't know what. And even worse, she believed Cassady didn't know, either.

Pauling continued to cruise down the highway, to the west. Her sleep had been brief, but solid. The coffee had woken her up, and she was excited to have turned in the babysitting part of the job for the actual investigation work.

It suited her better.

She'd gotten an idea of the location of the crime scene from the cops who'd arrived at Cassady's house.

It didn't take long for her to find the spot. There were several orange cones pulled off to the side of the road. Behind them were tire marks and loose debris. Out of the corner of her eye, far off in the desert, she thought she could see the flutter of crime scene tape.

Pauling pulled the car off the road and parked. She checked her cell phone to make sure she had a good signal and it was fully charged. Her gun was in its holster. She locked the car up, slipped the keys into her front pocket and began the hike across the desert to the spot where Rick Simmons had most likely been killed.

She couldn't be accused of tampering with a crime scene, as it was basically abandoned, and too big an area to keep contained. Plus, since it was the local cops who'd let slip the location of the crime, they wouldn't be in any kind of a big hurry to admit their mistake.

As she walked, Pauling had to admit that she didn't know exactly what she was looking for. Just trying to get a feel for what may have happened and why this location.

The morning sky was just beginning to turn from orange to blue, and the cool desert breeze felt good on her face. She'd put on trail running shoes and blue jeans, with a black t-shirt and light jacket. Her pistol was snug on her hip.

She spotted a small mound of dirt, a shallow depression, and the remains of two flags of crime scene tape.

This was the spot.

Where Cassady's husband met his fate.

She slowly approached the site of Rick Simmons' final resting place and scanned the area. Not much. A few scrub bushes, rocks and sand. A stand of cactus off to the north. A bird flew overhead, looking for a meal, no doubt.

Pauling knew the cops would leave the crime scene like this for the time being. Eventually, someone would come and take down the signs, after the investigation was over. Or maybe not. Maybe they'd leave it all for the desert to reclaim. Cassady might come out and somehow mark the spot with a cross.

Then again, Pauling didn't know if the young woman was strong enough for that kind of thing. Certainly not for awhile.

Pauling wondered about the time of the murder. She imagined the killers had waited to do it at night. Far from the road. They would have needed to eliminate the possibility of being seen by the occasional passing car. They were far enough from the city to the point where there was very little traffic. But there was enough that it would have been a factor to some degree.

The first insight she gained was that the killers were brazen.

They must have parked their car. But where? She walked back and studied the tire tracks. There were too many. She wondered if the cops had noticed the tracks.

Had the killers simply pulled their car off the road and parked on the shoulder? That would have taken some nerve. A parked car on the side of the highway at night? Say a cop just happened to cruise by and notice the vehicle. They would stop, jot down the license. Call it in. Proof that the car was there.

No, they would have driven the car all the way off the highway, into the desert, far enough from the road to make sure no one had seen them.

Which meant their tracks were in the sand.

Pauling hoped the cops had taken good photos of the tracks. They would possibly come in handy. She thought of the Crown Vic from Cassady's house. No way to tell if the tires were a match just looking at them.

The other thing about the crime scene was that it seemed sudden. Like, they hadn't had a good plan of where to take Rick Simmons.

It seemed like a location chosen by means of opportunity.

They grabbed him here, killed him here, and left him here.

It just didn't seem like the kind of place to dump bodies. Too close to the city. Not far enough from the road.

They had a huge desert to choose from, yet they chose this spot.

Maybe they were just lazy.

And not as professional as she might have first assumed.

The other mistake they made was that they hadn't dug the grave deep enough. The coyote found it. The plane saw it. It should have been dug much deeper with a lot more sand on it. And then some rocks should have been scattered on top. Big enough that a small mammal couldn't push the rocks off.

Again, maybe lazy.

Or maybe amateurs.

Or both.

Pauling stayed another twenty minutes,

walking and thinking, taking some photos of the scene for later examination and to confirm details.

She decided she'd gotten all she could, so Pauling started walking back to her car. When her vehicle was in sight, she saw another car drive by her rented Impala.

It was going at a slow, steady speed. Perhaps a bit slower than normal, which is what caught Pauling's attention.

It was past then, and sped up noticeably.

Pauling got a glimpse of two people in the car. One driver. One passenger.

She couldn't tell if they were men or women.

Or if they were the same two men who had tried to grab Cassady.

But the car was a Crown Vic.

Pauling considered chasing after them, but they had already crested the horizon by the time she got to her car and a high-speed chase would have been pointless.

Instead, she headed for Cassady's house.

And Michael Tallon.

38

"**I**s this what normal people do?" Tallon asked.

He was sitting in Cassady's living room. The bullet holes from the failed abduction were still visible, but he had cleaned up the plaster and dust on the floor.

Pauling had just arrived, fresh from her foray into the desert.

Tallon thought she looked especially good. Perfectly fitting blue jeans, a light cotton short-sleeved shirt and hiking shoes.

"Yeah, but most people have the television on," Pauling pointed out.

"I tried that but it was annoying," Tallon answered. "Much better this way. Quiet."

The couch was so soft he felt like he was sinking into it. Becoming a part of it.

"I read somewhere that the average person watches something like five hours a day of television," Tallon continued. "How is that even possible?"

"It's called binge-watching," Pauling said. "Where's Cassady?"

"She's in her room," Tallon said. "Crying."

He had tried to talk to her, but she wasn't very responsive. Tallon had figured that role might be better suited for Pauling, anyway.

"There's coffee," he added.

"Let me check on her first," Pauling said.

Tallon waited. He could smell Pauling's perfume. It was nice. Clean. Refreshing. A little citrus in there. Pauling was even better looking than he'd remembered. He wondered about her background with the FBI. He knew she'd handled some high-profile cases, even been involved with one that involved some mercenaries. The soldiers of fortune were people Tallon had known of vaguely, which was why the case had stuck with him, probably. He also recalled that was the situation where Jack Reacher had gotten involved.

Tallon had a feeling there'd been more

between Reacher and Pauling than just detective work. Something about the way she looked when Reacher's name was mentioned.

That thought was interrupted when Pauling came back out of Cassady's room.

"We need to talk," she said.

They each took up a corner of the kitchen table, a fresh cup of coffee now in front of Pauling.

"What did you find?" Tallon asked. "Anything the cops missed?"

He watched Pauling as she formulated her response.

"Death in the desert, and not much else," she said. "They found whatever they were going to find. It wasn't like I was going to come across a spent shell casing they'd overlooked or something. I just wanted to see where it happened."

She had a tablet and opened up the map app, tapped a few times with her finger and showed it to Tallon.

"Here's where it happened," she said. She set the tablet on the table and spun it around for Tallon to see.

He looked at the map.

"So we're here," he said. He put his finger near the location of Cassady's house.

"And she works here," Pauling said, pointing out Cassady's office building.

"What about the husband?" Tallon asked.

"He was a truck driver. Rio Grande Trucking," Pauling said. She dug through her notes from her first conversation with Cassady and came up with an address, which she copied down by hand.

She pushed it across the table to Tallon.

He called it up on the tablet and the three locations made a nice little triangle.

"Why don't you go check Rio Grande Trucking?" Pauling said. "I'll stay with her for the time being," Pauling said. "I'm not too worried about them coming for her again."

Tallon snatched up the address and headed for the door.

He wondered if Pauling would start getting some of her five hours of required television viewing in while he was gone.

Probably not.

Like him, she liked action.

And now, he was very glad to be back in action.

39

Tallon liked the tag-team approach. He'd done a fair amount of personal security jobs. They paid well but weren't his favorite task.

Usually, he felt like a babysitter with a gun.

So he was more than happy to let Pauling stay with the woman.

The house was secure. Pauling was good. He wasn't worried about it.

Tallon plugged Rio Grande Trucking's address into his phone's navigation and followed it west out of Albuquerque. He drove past a strip mall with a mega store, gas station and fast food restaurant.

Later on, he passed a mobile home dealership.

He realized he'd never seen a mobile home dealership. But of course there would be such a thing. It's not like people would buy them online.

A long stretch of desert followed until he came to an intersection where his navigation told him to turn.

He did so and found himself in front of an abandoned gas station. There was ancient plywood over the windows. The gas pumps were long gone, filled over with concrete. Scrub weeds were everywhere.

It had the look of a business that had gone belly up at least a decade or two ago.

Tallon parked and looked at the ghostly setting in front of him.

If Rio Grande Trucking existed, this certainly wasn't it. There was no way this place had been in existence until a few weeks ago.

This enterprise had gone out of business a long time ago.

He texted Pauling and asked her to confirm the address, which she did. She even said it was the correct address according to the business information listed on the Internet, which they both knew didn't mean a lot. But still. For some reason, this address was linked with Rio Grande Trucking.

Now curious, Tallon got out of his vehicle and walked up to the door. There was some graffiti, and it looked like someone had tried to pry the door open, to no avail. Litter was strewn around but looked like most of it had been investigated and discarded by the local rodent population.

Tallon walked around to the side of the building.

Everything was gone.

The foundation for a small air conditioning unit was there, but the unit itself had been removed, along with any piping and electrical conditions. Anything of scrap value looked like it had been severed with a cutting instrument, probably a reciprocating saw. The kind that goes through wood and metal.

Not stolen, just methodically removed with very little effort at conservation. Which told Tallon this was possibly a bankruptcy and foreclosure situation. Parts stripped off for what little money the bank could get.

In the rear of the building was a small parking lot, a few spaces probably for the employees, and maybe a few for repaired cars or two.

Not a very ambitious parking lot. Maybe that

lack of purpose was one of the reasons the place had gone kaput.

All of the parking spaces were empty now. Just cracked asphalt. Loose gravel. And weeds.

Tallon had quickly dismissed the idea that Rick Simmons had been working here until recently. There was no Rio Grande Trucking here. Maybe they'd moved. He thought about calling Pauling and seeing if there was perhaps another Rio Grande Trucking. But he figured she was a pro and would have already done that.

He stood looking at the sad sight in front of him.

It was all wrong for a trucking company, too. They would need a big loading dock. Places to park the big rigs. Sure, there was plenty of empty space around, but not the kind a trucking company would need. Even if it was a tiny company, say, with only a truck or two. This still wouldn't fit the bill.

Tallon continued his walk around the building. Above a side door he spotted an under-mounted black dome of glass. Small, just big enough for a camera. Probably disconnected and not powered.

Still, a little odd the dome of glass hadn't been smashed. It looked like the area was home to more than a few vandals. Everything else had been pretty much torn away, covered up, or left in ruin.

Tallon thought about the idea of a fake address being used for Rio Grande Trucking.

In his experience, fake addresses were a lot like fake names.

Often, they held a clue to the truth. People on the run often chose a new identity using the same initials as their real name. John Smith became Joe Sullivan. That sort of thing.

Maybe this abandoned gas station had something to do with Rick Simmons' murder.

Then two things happened.

Pauling called and said that it was possible to take a different road from the address of Rio Grande Trucking to the area where Rick Simmons' body had been found. A shortcut of sort. Not only was it a straight shot, but it meant the distance between the two locations was less than a mile. Which seemed like a huge coincidence to Pauling.

And it seemed that way to Tallon, too.

The other thing he realized was a bit more immediate.

Tallon suddenly realized he wasn't alone.

40

"I have a question about Rick's job," Pauling said.

Cassady was flat on her back in bed. Her eyes were rimmed with red. A box of Kleenex was next to her. She had a pillow in her arms and was hugging it close to her body. Using it like an inadequate shield.

"What?" Cassady asked.

"Have you ever been to his job? His place of work?"

"He was a truck driver," Cassady said. "He didn't have an office. His cab was his place of work."

She sniffled and pushed a wad of Kleenex up against the base of her nose.

"Did he ever say anything about having to visit the company's office?" Pauling asked. "You know, like its headquarters?"

"No."

"What about paperwork?" Pauling asked. "Most truck companies have a physical office where they keep the paperwork, if nothing else. Did he ever say anything about having to drop off paperwork, or pick up a load. Anything like that?"

Cassady shook her head. A flash of irritation crossed her face.

"What does this have to do with what happened?" Cassady said. She sounded angry, and Pauling realized a lot of the emotion was simple fatigue and shock. Mixed together with a devastating depression.

"Why are you asking me about this? He was a truck driver," Cassady said. "Nobody does this to somebody because they drive a truck."

Pauling decided not to tell her what Tallon had found. Not yet, anyway.

"I guess I was just wondering if he ever had to go and meet with a boss. Or a secretary. Or a dispatcher or something like that. Was there ever a reason he had to go to the physical office of Rio Grande Trucking?"

"Nope. Never," Cassady said.

Like everything else on this case, it was a dead end. Was there a Rio Grande Trucking? Had Rick made the whole thing up? If so, who did he work for? And who did he work with?

"Did he ever talk about anyone at work? Any names? Any coworkers?" she asked. Her voice betrayed the incredibly low odds of receiving a positive response. It was a long shot, through and through.

Now the irritation in Cassady's face morphed into something else.

"Sandy." Cassady said it with far too much emotion.

"Sandy?" Pauling replied. "Who's Sandy?"

Cassady waved a hand clutching a Kleenex like she was dismissing the thought.

"I assumed it was a dispatcher or something," she said. "Somebody who would actually have a reason to talk with the drivers," Cassady said.

Pauling caught the undercurrent of emotion.

"Rick didn't say who she was?"

"Nope."

It was definitely not adding up. Pauling decided to press the issue.

"He just said her name? Without any context?"

Cassady's mouth narrowed to a severe, thin line. She turned to Pauling and her eyes cleared, shining with an intensity that hadn't been there before.

"Yeah," Cassady. "In his sleep."

41

"Help you?"

Tallon turned and saw two men watching him.

They were both big in their own way. One was very tall, at least 6'6" with a pear-shaped body. The other was average height but twice as wide as his partner. His shoulders were massive, his arms were thick, but very short. A wrestler, not a puncher. The tall one would be the striker. He would fire from a distance allowing the other one to get in close.

If it came to that.

They wore jeans, hiking boots and t-shirts. The short, wide one had on a baseball cap. Tallon thought of the term 'shit-kicker' and how it was highly applicable here.

The short, stocky guy was also the one who'd spoken.

Tallon slid his phone into his front pocket, having just finished talking with Pauling. The men must have pulled up quietly and parked behind Tallon's vehicle.

"You deaf?"

That was the tall one. He had a high-pitched voice. Not in the least intimidating. In fact, Tallon smiled at the sound of it.

It was like being threatened by Pee-Wee Herman.

The two men shifted slightly, putting more room between them.

"So the camera works?" Tallon asked. He'd noticed the little dome of dark glass, that it was the only thing that looked like it survived. Which had been odd. Considering the general decrepit state of everything else. His suspicions had clearly been confirmed.

Neither guy answered.

"What do you guys do, sit together in some little office somewhere, keeping close tabs on the abandoned gas station?" Tallon said with a laugh.

"That's what your lives have come to? You must have been real stars in the classroom. Do you jerk each other off if someone shows up here?"

His tone and attitude took them by surprise.

The tall one glanced down at the stocky one. Clearly, he was looking for his shorter counterpart to take the lead.

The stocky one pulled out an extendable baton and snapped it all the way open with a flick of his wrist.

Tallon almost smiled.

The gesture was meant to scare him. To fill him with terror. Maybe make him submissive and do what they asked.

It had the opposite effect.

For a couple of reasons.

One, the extendable baton as a weapon was best used to disarm someone. Slashing strikes downward that connected with bone, wrist or fingers, designed to knock a weapon from someone's grip was the best way to use it. That's what it had been designed for. A lot of would-be toughs didn't know that, of course. They tended to use it the incorrect way. Trying to clobber someone over the head, for instance. Something told Tallon that the man in front of him hadn't done his homework. In fact, he'd probably never done any home-work, ever.

Tallon had yet to draw a weapon.

Two, an extendable baton was a good way to keep distance from a potential threat. Again, that was the impetus for its creation in the first place. If the tall one had the baton, it would be even better. Very difficult for Tallon to strike the tall man with his long arms, extended even farther with the baton.

Now, the instrument also had some disadvan-tages. It required a good amount of energy to wind up and unleash a strike. It could be used to jab, but that wasn't the best move.

The only way their current setup would work was if Tallon attacked the stocky man with a weapon extended in front of him.

He wasn't about to do that.

However, getting in close first to the guy with the baton was the way to go.

"This is going to be fun," the baton-wielding man said.

And then they made their move.

The tall one came in first and the move revealed the plan. The tall one would attack with a long-distance punch, and the stocky guy would pound Tallon with the baton while he fought with the big guy.

Tallon's reaction was instantaneous.

He launched himself at the stocky one who attempted to draw back the baton in a big sweeping strike.

Wrong move and he was both way too slow and way too late.

Tallon's straight kick caught him in the solar plexus and the man seemed to momentarily hang in the air as the power and viciousness of the kick left him stunned, gasping for air.

The baton's backswing stopped and the stocky man's upper body leaned forward. Tallon's momentum carried him forward and he drove a straight right into the middle of the man's face, squashing the nose and driving the cartilage back and upward, directly into the frontal lobe of the man's brain.

He flew backward, falling on his back and his skull made a loud cracking sound as it hit the asphalt.

The baton flew from the man's hand and Tallon caught it with his right hand, still on the follow through from the terrific blow he'd just delivered. He turned on his heel, pivoted his hips and swung the baton.

The tall man was still coming, too late to adjust his course, and the baton hit him in the neck, just under the jaw line. Its knobbed end drove into the nerves of the tall man's spine. His eyes rolled over to white, and his body jolted like he'd stepped on a live wire.

Tallon brought the baton back, twisting the other way in a backhand with a short arc that connected with the tall man's temple.

It was a terrible blow and the man tottered, as if he was checking his shoelaces, and then he fell face-first into the blacktop.

In some states, Tallon knew that an extendable baton used to strike the head area was considered lethal force in a court of law.

Oh well.

Self-defense was a beautiful thing.

Tallon used his shirt to wipe off the handle of the baton, and he threw it into the distance of the parking lot where it rolled into a clump of weeds.

The whole process had taken less than thirty seconds and in the meantime, no one else had driven by the area.

Tallon approached the stocky man and put his fingers to the man's throat.

He was dead.

Tallon relieved the man of his wallet and went to his partner, who was clearly still breathing. Tallon took his wallet, too. He went to his vehicle, noted his opponents had arrived in a Crown Vic.

Wasn't that what Pauling had said the men who tried to grab Cassady had been driving?

Tallon climbed into his vehicle and drove away.

42

C assady was no longer any help.

Pauling recognized that.

There always came a time when a witness or family member could no longer contribute anything meaningful to an investigation. They had been wrung for any and all information. Any new insights would only come with brand-new questions. But those would have to come later, when new information arrived that prompted new questions.

So when the person was no longer a resource, and when that person was also in danger, there were two approaches.

One, use them as bait.

Two, get them to a safe house.

Pauling had a hotel room. It would only be considered a safe room for Cassady if she or Tallon were there, too. It would provide no protection to stash Cassady there and leave her by herself. So, guarding her at the hotel was really no different than guarding her at the house. If the bad guys knew to come here, they could probably figure out where Pauling was.

Using Cassady as bait, on the other hand, wasn't a bad idea. A tried and true technique. Sometimes the bait was killed, however.

Also, they had tried once to grab Cassady and failed. The odds of them trying again were slim. Sure, they could assemble a huge strike force but Pauling didn't think that would be the case. Especially now that the bad guys knew Cassady was being guarded.

The other thing Pauling hated about using her client as bait was that it was a passive approach. She hated taking a passive angle on an investigation. It was always, for her, the last resort. Only used after she'd exhausted every other avenue. Being active was the key. Pushing forward, always seeking progress.

Sure, there were times when you had to play a

waiting game. But this wasn't one of them. At least, not now.

She, Pauling, was a very good investigator, if she thought so herself. So was Tallon. Using either one as a bodyguard was a misallocation of resources, in Bureau terminology.

No, she needed to be actively solving the case.

Having a third person was a luxury she couldn't afford. It was always a possibility, Pauling had been in charge of teams numbering in the dozens. But this case, she was only here because of Reacher. Or his name, more accurately. If it hadn't been splashed across the front of that envelope, she would have ignored Cassady Simmons and her plight.

Instead, she came out here, hoping to see Reacher.

And now, she was working a case pro bono. Which was a fancy way of saying she was working for free.

Which meant she needed to wrap this thing up, but like everything else that was easier said than done.

Tallon interrupted her train of thought with a text that he was here and about to enter the house.

Letting her know so his arrival didn't startle anyone. Namely, Cassady.

Pauling went to the door and let him in.

"How is she?" he asked.

"Sleeping," Pauling said and nodded her head toward the closed door of Cassady's bedroom.

"So are these guys," Tallon said, and handed her two wallets.

Pauling took them, and glanced at the IDs.

"What happened?" she said.

Pauling listened as Tallon walked her through the scene at the abandoned gas station. She found it particularly interesting the location was under surveillance, and that the two men were driving a Crown Vic.

"So not only did they publish a fake address for Rio Grande Trucking, they figured somebody would eventually come looking for it. Hence, the camera," Pauling said.

"Which means their plan wasn't very long-term," Tallon said.

"Good point," Pauling said. The long-term play would have been to make sure no one ever came looking. By putting up a camera, they had pretty much planned somebody would be investigating.

Which meant they were working on a limited time frame."

"I killed one of them, just so you know," Tallon said.

He said it with about as much emotion as someone stating there were leftovers in the fridge.

"Was the other one mobile?" Pauling asked.

"Not right away," he answered. "But he's probably awake by now."

"They won't go to the cops," Pauling said. "They have the camera so they watched it all. Probably sent a clean-up team the minute you left."

She thought it interesting the lack of reaction on Tallon's face. That was one thing he and Reacher had in common. They never went looking for trouble but if someone came at them, they didn't mind levying a very high price.

"Let's see what I can find on these names," Pauling said. She took the wallets to her computer and spent a few minutes accessing her databases remotely.

"Whoever they were, they certainly weren't the A-Team," Tallon said. "More like the C-minus team."

"Local help, most likely," Pauling said. "Hired cheap."

"Overconfident, too. Bringing your wallets to a beat down."

Pauling scanned the information her programs had recovered. "Yep," she said. "Locals. Minor criminal histories. No signs of employment. Free-lance thugs."

"You get what you pay for."

Pauling snapped her laptop shut and looked at Tallon.

He raised an eyebrow.

"You look like you have a plan," he said.

"I do," she answered. "Here's what we're going to do."

43

"Mr. Walker, I'm afraid Brooks is dead," the tall man said.

The bald man with the bulging veins kept his face impassive. They stood in the underground room, with a window looking into the chamber where the experiments took place. There was a person in restraints, most of his skin gone, and blood splattered around the floor.

"I know Brooks is dead," Walker said. "I watched him die."

Walker had made sure to put a surveillance camera on the gas station, just in case anyone started poking around about Rio Grande Trucking, after the disappearance of Rick Simmons. The world was full of people asking questions. The problem was, they were usually asking the wrong questions.

"So you saw it all?" the tall man said, his high-pitched voice sounding squeaky to his boss. Walker thought the big man sounded like a mouse. An overgrown mouse.

"Of course I did," Walker said. "The joy of seeing you two morons getting your asses kicked was negated by the realization of how severely I've overpaid you."

A vein on the side of the bald man's head was throbbing, and the tall man knew that was a bad sign.

"I've got Brooks' body in the car. Want me to throw it in the incinerator?"

Walker shook his head.

"Not yet. Go get that one first," he said, nodding toward the dead test subject in the chamber. "Throw both of them in there together and then meet me up at the command center. We've got to make some moves and make them fast."

The tall man was buoyed by his boss's forgiveness. He opened the door to the chamber and went to the chair. He wondered about putting on some protective gear but he was afraid to ask.

Behind him, he heard the door slam shut and the heavy locking mechanism rammed into place.

Above him, he heard a gurgle of liquid begin heading toward the shower head.

"No!" he shouted.

He ran back to the door and heaved on it, but he knew firsthand it was impregnable. He'd watched many unfortunate souls do what he was doing just then.

The fluid erupted from the shower head and began spraying in a 360 degree pattern. It splashed onto his face and hands igniting a burning pain the kind he'd never experienced before.

On the other side of the glass, Walker watched the tall man screaming at him.

He smiled.

"Another mouse dies in the name of science," he said and laughed.

44

Chicago. That's where Pauling's plan started.

She had a friend, a nurse, who specialized in obstetrics. Pauling knew she could stash Cassady there, safely.

Pauling had a long history of investigation and over that time had developed a sixth sense for when it was time to get one's hands dirty.

Now was the time.

Just to be sure, she booked a flight out of Phoenix for Cassady, instead of Albuquerque, just in case anyone was watching the airport. Who knew? Someone had put a camera at an abandoned gas station. Having a watcher at the airport wasn't out of the question.

Pauling was confident they wouldn't be watching in Phoenix, though.

"Why do I have to leave again?" Cassady said. She sat on the edge of her bed, her shoulders slumped.

"It won't be for long," Pauling assured her. "Just a few days, probably, until we get this thing sorted out."

"What about my work?"

"We'll have you call in sick. Do you have sick time?"

Cassady nodded.

"Okay, that's what we'll do."

Pauling hugged Cassady and handed her an envelope. "There's three thousand dollars in here in cash. Keep it on you. It's yours. Don't worry about it."

"What about the police, though? They said I should tell them if I planned to travel anywhere."

"I have to talk to them anyway," Pauling said. "I'll let them know you stepped out for a bit but that you'll be back in a few days. It won't be a problem."

"Okay," Cassady said.

She looked around the house and Pauling knew what she was thinking. That this had been her home. Where she thought she was going to raise a family.

Instead, she was left alone.

"Make sure she gets on the plane safely," Pauling said to Tallon.

"You got it," he said.

Tallon and Cassady left and Pauling wondered about the local cops. About how exactly she would handle that. She'd told Cassady she would take care of it.

It was mostly true.

She just didn't know *when* she would share Cassady's whereabouts.

Pauling locked up Cassady's house and drove down to her hotel room, showered, changed, and thought about her next steps.

Tallon would be back once Cassady was safely on the plane.

In the meantime, her plan was to dig deeper on the IDs of the men Tallon had dealt with at the abandoned gas station. She'd already run the basics through her software programs, but was waiting for information from one of her backchannel searches. The kind that didn't appear in normal Internet traffic and therefore couldn't be traced.

A message was waiting in her inbox telling her that the information had arrived. She scanned through it, noting that it contained most of what she'd already learned.

With one exception.

Employment.

In her initial background search, it had showed both men were unemployed. But this database, a back door into the IRS, traced payments to both men from an entity called S & S Security.

What really caught Pauling's eye, though, was the address associated with S & S Security. It was the same as Rio Grande Trucking.

The exact same address as Rio Grande Trucking.

Which Pauling already knew was an abandoned gas station west of the city.

Reacher, what did you get me into? Pauling wondered. *More accurately, what had Rick Simmons been into? Why him?*

She stood and began to pace. Sometimes, she thought better on her feet.

What would Reacher do? He would explore the avenues. Think about who stood to gain. There were always commonalities. Cornerstone motivations at the root of most evil done by mankind.

So far, Pauling had been unable to find out who would want to target Rick Simmons. And his wife.

There had been no financial problems.

No extramarital affairs.

Except for a mysterious coworker named Sandy, whose name had been whispered during the night. Not much to go on. Certainly not much to take to the cops.

Plus, Cassady was pregnant.

The more she thought about it, the more she felt Rick Simmons was the key. Cassady was just a distraction. Or maybe insurance.

Rick's story was tied up with Rio Grande Trucking, which shared an address with two thugs in a Crown Vic.

Pauling's thoughts returned to Sandy.

How could she find the woman if she couldn't even find the company itself? Pauling paced and thought. She rolled her head from side to side. She wished Reacher was there to provide some physical distraction.

But he wasn't.

Well, one option would be to call every trucking company in Albuquerque and ask for Sandy. See if anyone answered in the positive. And then what? Ask Sandy if she knew a Rick Simmons who might have mentioned her name in his sleep? Sandy would probably know that Rick was missing. Maybe Sandy was missing too. Or maybe she was involved.

It was a horrible plan, but it was all she had. So Pauling spent the next three hours calling every trucking company in the Albuquerque area.

There was no one named Sandy.

She went down to the hotel's café and ordered a coffee. She was tempted to add a brownie out of frustration but decided against it.

Without Sandy, the only other thing that stood out to her about this case was Reacher. Why was his name used? Who wrote it on the envelope? Why was it sent to her?

What did she know about Reacher that might apply to this case?

He was former Army. An MP often placed in charge of homicide investigations. He was a tough guy who hated to see injustice done. Who tended to stand up for those who were being bullied.

Everything about Reacher screamed ex-military.

For some reason, the word 'military' resonated with Pauling.

She felt something akin to a vibration.

The military.

How did the military and Albuquerque interact? What would have involved Reacher out here?

Pauling's jaw suddenly dropped open.

"Oh my God," she said out loud. Much louder than she expected because several people in the hotel coffee shop turned to look at her.

She jumped to her feet and headed for her room, dialing Tallon on her phone.

Why hadn't she seen it sooner?

Suddenly, she knew *exactly* who Sandy was.

45

"Any chance you're going to tell us what the hell is going on?" the man with the thinning blond hair and ruddy complexion asked Agent Hess. They were in a conference room in the Albuquerque FBI office. Ostertag was at the head of the table. To his right was an older man with perfectly combed gray hair. To his left, a Hispanic man with thick black glasses.

Hess sat at the other end of the table.

"I can tell you some of what we know," she replied. "But there's a reason we were alerted back in DC, instead of you."

"Yeah, that's what I figured," Ostertag said, his voice thick with sarcasm. "I get a call that some hotshot agent from HQ is coming out here and I have to have a team assembled. No indication what it's about. You know, we've got our own stuff to deal with here. We've got a huge ring of meth dealers. A truck full of illegal immigrants was found yesterday. They were all dead. Nine bodies roasting in the desert like meat in an oven."

Hess let out a slow breath.

"I appreciate your current responsibilities," she said. "I've been given strict instructions to ensure the reason I'm here today receives your top priority."

Ostertag rolled his eyes. He was an impatient man, Hess could see. "Of course it is. That's why we're here."

"It starts with a man named Rick Simmons," Hess said.

Ostertag shook his head, and looked at the other two men in the room. They gave him blank looks.

"Never heard of him," Ostertag said.

"Well, you won't be hearing anything," Hess said. "Because he's dead. Murdered in the desert yesterday."

"Okay," Ostertag said.

"He was a truck driver. Working for a company called Rio Grande Trucking."

Ostertag's irritated demeanor instantly vanished.

"Oh shit," he said.

Hess smiled at him. "Exactly."

46

"Sandia," Pauling said to Tallon. "As in Sandia Nuclear Laboratories."

"The nuke guys? What about them?" he answered.

Pauling relayed the conversation she'd had with Cassady. The one where she said Rick Simmons had been talking about 'Sandy' in his sleep.

"That's it?" he asked. "You think just because he's a truck driver and he mentioned a Sandy that he was involved with the nukes?"

"Rick Simmons wasn't talking about a mysterious Sandy," Pauling said. "He was talking about Sandia. His real employer."

"Sandia uses truck drivers? I thought they built nuclear missiles. A bunch of geeky scientists and stuff."

"They do both."

They were sitting at a table in the coffee shop of Pauling's hotel. Tallon was back from dropping off Cassady, without incident. He was hungry and had ordered two ham and cheese croissant sandwiches with black coffee.

"Nothing like microwaved bread," he said as they were delivered. He had devoured both of the sandwiches in minutes, after offering Pauling one. She had declined.

Pauling thought he looked eager. Babysitting didn't sit well with him, either apparently.

"What do you mean both? They do all the scientific stuff and they truck the shit around the country? That seems dangerous."

"That's why they do it themselves," Pauling explained.

"For security reasons," Tallon said.

"Right. They can't subcontract trucking with something like that. Could you imagine the public outcry if they found out some joe-trucking-operation-off-the-street was hauling around nuclear material? Maybe the guy takes a break at a truck stop, gets a prostitute and dies. The hooker drives off with a load of nukes."

"Yeah, that wouldn't be good," Tallon said. "Hookers and nuclear warheads are a bad combination. Trust me." He smiled at Pauling.

"How much do you know about Sandia?" she asked him.

"Just that they do the nuke stuff. Related to the Manhattan Project, right? Had a role in building the A-bomb?"

"Right, sort of," Pauling said. She sat back in her chair and studied Tallon. "Let me give you what I know. It's not everything, but for our purposes, it will do. Sandia National Laboratories was developed a little after Los Alamos. Los Alamos – where they built the bomb, needed a place to build non-nuclear materials that supported their efforts. It was decided to keep them separate. Thus, Sandia was born. Eventually, they became involved in nuclear operations, too, all in support of Los Alamos."

"So you're telling me Sandia has a fake address? And a camera? The goons are from the government?" Tallon asked. He drained the rest of his coffee, glanced at Pauling. She didn't want anymore, anyway. She was pumped. This was progress.

Pauling shook her head. "No. Sandia is not bush-league. The gas station, the guys you dealt with, all scream locals. Someone locally planted that address. Sandia has probably never heard of Rio Grande Trucking. This whole Rick Simmons angle was probably a surprise to them, too. They're a major military player. Which is probably how Jack Reacher is mixed up in all of this."

"Yeah, what's the deal with Reacher?" Tallon asked. "What's his story, anyway? Where is he?"

"I keep wondering that, too," Pauling said. "At least now I know why he was involved. This is exactly the kind of thing he would get mixed up in. But, for now, we've got to move forward assuming that Rick Simmons was driving for Sandia. And he was killed. And whoever killed him, wanted Cassady for something."

"For what, though? That's the big question," Tallon said. "It's not like Cassady Simmons is walking around with nuclear codes or something."

"No, that isn't the big question," Pauling answered.

"What is?"

She sighed. "Where in the hell is Rick Simmons' truck?"

47

"So this Rick Simmons is dead?" Ostertag asked.

"That's correct," Hess said. "Shot in the desert. And buried. Although they were thorough in killing him, they weren't so fastidious in the burial process. A coyote dug him up, and then a plane spotted the body in the desert."

"What about the truck?"

"Well, that's where it gets interesting. How much do you know about the trucks used to deploy nuclear materials?"

Ostertag glanced around the room. No one volunteered to admit their lack of knowledge. "I know a little bit. There are a couple of factories that make the bombs, and then they have to be delivered. Usually to air force bases. I'd heard the trucks had armed guards and such. Was that not the case?"

Hess smiled at him. "Very good. However, these trucks usually have a lot more security measures than armed guards. Typically, there's an additional armed guard in the cab with the driver, who is also armed. There's usually a tail vehicle. If it's a really big delivery, there might be a lead car as well. But that's not all. The truck itself, even though it looks pretty much like your average tractor trailer, is loaded with electronic gear. Satellite-based GPS devices. Remote access driver controls."

"Then how the hell...?" one of the agents asked.

"Additionally, there are small explosive charges placed at the wheels," Hess said. "Should the driver determine it necessary, he can literally blow the wheels off the trailer, rendering it completely immobile."

"What about the tracking devices then?" Ostertag said. "If it was designed to avoid all of this, we should know exactly where it is."

"The internal security team at Sandia doesn't

know what happened, either. But they're cooperating," Hess said. "They called us in."

"Local police?" an agent said.

"Cooperating as well," Hess said. "We already knew Rick Simmons was missing, so as soon as they got the call, we intervened. No problems there. They know all about Sandia and Los Alamos. They know where their bread is buttered. No territorial pissing matches here. The only issue is a lack of evidence. No one's got anything so far."

"So what are we doing now?" Ostertag asked.

"We've got to pursue this thing 24/7. Rick Simmons had a wife, Cassady Simmons, who somehow managed to hire a private investigator before we got involved. I need someone to handle that situation," Hess said. "Ostertag, you and your team also need to work the local angles. Everyone here knows someone involved with military industries north and west of here. It's not so much a question of who would have taken the material. It's more, who would have the intelligence and the capability to even deal with it. This isn't a bunch of M-13 gang-bangers we're dealing with. There has to be at least a baseline of knowledge to understand what they're dealing with. See what you can find out."

"I'm still having trouble understanding how a semi-truck full of nuclear material could simply vanish," Ostertag said.

It was the obvious question, and Hess hesitated to speculate, but providing a good answer would help the team focus.

"Most likely, there was cooperation from the team. Maybe the driver. Maybe additional folks. Essentially, carjacking a nuclear truck is impossible. It could have only been done with someone helping from the inside. The question is, why? What was their motivation to steal a truck full of nukes?" she said.

One of the more junior agents at the table cleared his throat.

"I'm sure there are other people here wondering the same thing. But I have to ask, just so I know what kind of threat we're talking about." He glanced down at the notepad in front of him, as if he was afraid to ask the question while making direct eye contact with Hess.

"So what kind of payload did Simmons have in his truck?"

Ostertag nearly winced at the directness of the question.

He looked around at his team, who were also suddenly studying the notepads in front of them.

Finally, he glanced at Hess.

She shrugged her shoulders and answered with a tone that was casually informative.

"Enough to wipe out most of California."

48

"I knew a military guy who drove a nuke truck. He was a bad ass. Told me all about the vehicle," Tallon said.

He and Pauling were parked a half mile from the entrance to Sandia Labs. It was the closest they could get, a mega gas station barely in sight of the entrance to the complex. They'd had to buy waters and snacks to justify staying in the parking lot. Before long, they would be noticed.

"Yep. I did some research on those suckers. It's like Fort Knox on wheels," Pauling said. "They look like civilian vehicles, but they're 100% military grade. Total defensive measures, including the axles being wired with explosives to blow the wheels off so no one can drive off with it."

"Didn't work, apparently," Tallon said.

"Rick Simmons wasn't ex-military, though," Pauling pointed out. "Or at least he told his wife he wasn't. Maybe he was lying and he did some time in the Army. Maybe that's how Reacher was involved," Pauling said.

"Could be," Tallon admitted. "How many drivers does Sandia have?"

"I don't know," Pauling said. "Probably not that many. But Sandia is just one operator within the whole nuclear program. There are probably a dozen fleets of trucks, driving all over the United States with nuclear material. From factories to military bases, to nuclear waste sites."

"That's my point then," Tallon said. "Multiple trucking operators. Multiple sites, right? A fleet of hundreds of trucks? That means there are hundreds of drivers and assorted personnel. It's not like Rick Simmons was the only one in charge of one of these rigs."

"No, I'm sure you're right. Lots of drivers. Lots of guards. Lots of support personnel. Could you imagine the risks involved?" Pauling asked. "What if one of these was driving through an ice storm and slid off the road?"

"They must have all kinds of emergency procedures in place."

"And they've probably planned for a scenario where someone tries to steal a truck. It would be a terrorist's wet dream," she said, looking at Tallon. "Why were you estimating the number of drivers?"

"Well, in addition to the question of where his truck is, I can't stop thinking about something else. Why Rick Simmons?"

"Nothing has jumped out at us," Pauling said.

"Usually you find some kind of weak link," Tallon said. "Drug addiction. Alcohol. Gambling. Prostitution. Affairs. We didn't find out anything about the guy. Other than the fact that he's got a pregnant wife who loves him very much."

Pauling was about to answer when a semi-truck pulled out of the side gate of the Sandia complex.

A white pickup truck was in front of it.

A plain sedan was behind it.

"So they have their security caravan in place," Tallon said. "I wonder if Rick Simmons had one? And if he did, how in the hell did they get the truck from him?"

"Or, how did they get him to cooperate? Give them the truck and what? Send him on his way?"

They were in Pauling's car, but Tallon was driving and he waited until the convoy was on the road and then he put the Impala in gear and followed.

He was good at being subtle in his approach to the truck.

But apparently, not subtle enough.

Not more than two miles into the pursuit, a siren erupted behind them, and Tallon was forced to pull off the road.

A plain sedan was behind them.

A man in a suit and tie walked up to the car. Tallon watched him, making sure his hands were out in the open. He rolled down the window.

"FBI," the man said and he showed Tallon his ID, which was legit.

The FBI man slid into the backseat of Pauling's car.

"Thanks for the ID, but I know a Feebie when I see one," Pauling said.

"Lauren Pauling," the man said. "Good to meet you. I'm Ray Ostertag. SAC of Albuquerque. Officially asking you to stand down. We are on the case."

"What case would that be?" Pauling asked.

"The same case you came out here for. Cassady Simmons. Her murdered husband."

"Let's not forget his missing truck," Tallon chimed in.

"I'm not going to ask again," Ostertag said. "We've got a lot of eyes on this thing."

"I can imagine," Pauling said. "It really wouldn't hurt, though, to have some extra intelligence to keep the bosses in Washington happy. We can help you out. Free of charge."

"No, absolutely not," Ostertag said. "Appreciate the offer, but we've got this. Rick Simmons is our problem now."

"Well, if you change your mind," Pauling said. She had her business card in hand and offered it to Ostertag.

He ignored it, opened the back door and got out, then stuck his head back in before closing the door.

"I won't ask again," he said and slammed the door shut.

49

"I have an idea," Pauling said.

"Let's hear it."

"The idea starts with a question."

"Shoot."

"If Rick Simmons had a truckload of nuclear material someone killed him for, why, after they killed Rick and apparently stole his truck, would they then go after Cassady? Didn't they already have what they wanted?"

Tallon played along. "Maybe she knew something. She could have blown the whistle on them. Sure, they already had what they wanted, but maybe they wanted to make sure they could get away with it, too."

"Maybe," Pauling said.

"But you don't think so?"

"Could be. Or not. My idea is, since we've been warned off of pursuing Rick Simmons, why not turn our attention back to Cassady?"

"Because we just stashed her hundreds of miles away," Tallon said. "If you recall, I personally drove her to the Phoenix airport and put her on a plane to Chicago."

"I'm not talking about questioning her again," Pauling said. "We tried that and got nowhere. That well has run dry. She can't *tell* us anything more. So we'll have to learn what we can without her now. But I also wonder if we were asking the wrong questions."

"What do you mean?"

"Well, we were looking at reasons why someone would want to kidnap Rick. But we never asked about her. Specifically, would someone use Rick to get to Cassady?"

Tallon nodded. "Yeah, I never really looked at it that way. It was either Rick. Or Rick and Cassady. Never just Cassady."

Pauling felt a surge of excitement. Intuition. Something felt right about this. Like when a puzzle couldn't be solved, realizing it wasn't the puzzle itself, but one's approach that was all wrong.

"Where did you say she worked?" Tallon asked.

"Industrial Supply & Wholesale. Why?"

"Honestly, there was nothing to Cassady personally," he said. "No family in the area. Pregnant. And if she was faking all of that drama over her missing husband, she deserves an Academy Award. Hell, the one for Lifetime Achievement, because she played that role to the hilt."

"Look, we're five minutes from her employer," Pauling said. "I know exactly where it is because that's where I met her the first time. Let's see what we can find out in person, and then we'll go from there."

Pauling directed Tallon and as they drove, Tallon said, "Plus what's great about this approach is we're not disobeying that FBI guy's orders. He told us not to pursue the Rick Simmons angle. See?" he said. "We're the epitome of well-behaved citizens."

"Sounds good to me," Pauling said, as they arrived at the building from which Cassady Simmons had emerged just days before. To Pauling, it seemed like a long time ago.

They went inside and told the woman at the front desk they were looking for some information regarding one of their employees. The receptionist asked them to wait. Fifteen minutes later, a woman appeared.

She was overweight, with red hair that had been put back into a bun but had now started to fray.

"I'm Debbie Macomb, Head of Human Resources here at ISW," she said. "I understand you have some questions about an employee. You must understand that any information of that nature is private."

Pauling got the impression the woman was off-script and not happy about it. She guessed Human Resources personnel weren't asked to improvise very often.

"Yes, I understand that, but this is a very important matter," Pauling said. She handed the woman her business card, where FBI was featured prominently.

Debbie Macomb seemed to consider it and then she said, "There's a small conference room down the hall, let's talk in there."

She led them to the room which featured a small round table, four chairs, and a plant in the corner. Its leaves were drooping and covered in dust.

"I can only provide information to you that is already public. Nothing that is confidential to the company. With that in mind, please go ahead and ask your questions. I'll do my best to be helpful."

"OK, we appreciate that," Pauling said. "I guess for starters, what does ISW do?"

"We supply a variety of products and services to the healthcare industry."

"Is this the only office or do you have other locations?"

"This is headquarters and the only office," Macomb said.

"How many employees?"

"A little over two hundred as of the start of the year."

Pauling was trying to keep a rhythm to the interview. Keeping the questions easy to answer and hopefully let the woman relax.

"Are you an independent company?"

"Yes."

"Owned by an individual? Or a holding company?"

"Our parent company is called Vanguard Holdings. This is all public information. And as much as I want to help, I have a meeting in five minutes. Is there anything else I can do for you?"

"Well, I'm not sure if you're aware of this but there's been a tragedy. I'm not at liberty to go into the details," Pauling said. "However, if there's anything you could do to help me understand more about Cassady Simmons and her time here, that would be great."

Debbie stood up.

"I'm afraid I have another meeting scheduled, and that is definitely not information I can provide. Sorry. I wish you luck in your efforts. Now, I'm afraid I'll have to escort you out of the building.

She didn't wait for a reply, and ushered them first from the conference room and then out the front door.

Pauling looked at Tallon.

"Was it just me or did she become anxious once the name Vanguard Holdings came up?"

"Definitely," he answered. "Right after it was mentioned, she suddenly had an urgent meeting."

Pauling started walking back toward the Impala.

"Let's see what we can find out about Vanguard Holdings."

50

Vance Walker loved globes. He loved looking at the world, miniaturized.

He didn't know why. At one point, he'd amassed a fairly large collection of expensive, antique globes.

And then he'd set them all on fire as he watched with a dry martini in hand.

There was only one he spared. A miniature that sat on his desk. Nothing valuable about it. He'd just liked having it on his desk.

Now, he watched it.

Imagined it with a population reduced by 99 percent.

The thought electrified him.

His cell phone rang and he looked at the screen, and then answered.

"Yes," he said.

The voice on the other end of the line spoke for some time. The person described the current situation and provided a best guess on the timing of certain logistical realities.

"I see," Walker said.

They spoke for several more minutes, and discussed an area near the western border before disconnecting.

Walker got to his feet.

Many, many years had brought him to this point in time and he wouldn't have done it any other way. It was his vision that had created a new reality. Changing the world required that sort of single-mindedness, guided by proprietary knowledge. No one else had it and even if they did, they wouldn't know what to do with it.

Now, he went to a hook next to the door to his private office and removed the shoulder holster equipped with a .45 semiautomatic handgun. He shrugged on the rig, and followed that with a light camouflage jacket.

He stepped outside and listened. There was the

hum of machinery, a few voices in the machine shop, and his armed guards near the entrance.

Walker found his second-in-command. A former Marine who'd lost a leg in Iraq and added a heroin addiction once he'd come back home.

He was clean now, and owed it all to Walker.

"Spread the word," Walker told him. "We're moving out in one hour. Make sure everyone follows the proper procedure. No mistakes."

With that done, Walker went down to the truck. It held everything he needed to begin what he considered to be his very own genesis. A fresh start. A chance to guide humankind back to the path from which it had deviated so long ago.

For the first time in his life, he could imagine a scenario in which human beings achieved their full potential.

Walker reached the oversized hangar door and breathed deeply. The scent of oil, gasoline and cigarette smoke filled the air.

Along with an excitement that hummed with more power than the multiple generators running in unison.

It was time, Walker thought.

His time.

51

Tallon again drove, as Pauling worked her iPad and phone.

"Okay, Vanguard Holdings," she said, reading aloud. "Headquarters are listed as Las Vegas, for obvious tax reasons, I'm guessing."

"And just think of how much more fun their holiday parties would be in Vegas, than here."

"Hmm, interesting," Pauling said. "Very difficult to find a publicly listed board of directors or executive leadership."

"Red flag," Tallon said.

Pauling picked up her phone. "I try not to use this source very much, but this calls for it."

She dialed a number and spoke briefly to

someone on the other end of the line. She waited. While doing so, she tapped away at the iPad.

"Yeah," she said into the phone, after several minutes of waiting.

"Vance Walker," she said, turning to Tallon. "Okay, thanks. I owe you a drink when you're in New York." Pauling laughed and disconnected from the call.

"I didn't know you buy drinks when people do you favors," Tallon said. "I would have exploited that a long time ago."

"Federal tax records show a man named Vance Walker is the owner of Vanguard Holdings," Pauling said. "Looks like he's a very wealthy man."

She was reading an article about Walker from several years ago. "Very wealthy."

Tallon tapped his fingers on the steering wheel. "Sure, those medical inventors make millions, as long as they hold the original patent, right? Every time someone uses their widget, they get a cut. It can add up, especially considering what hospitals charge nowadays."

"The question is, what, if anything, a medical company might have to do with a truck driver hauling around nuclear materials," Pauling wondered.

"Do hospitals use nuclear stuff? For tests or something?"

"Not that I know of. Maybe X-rays."

"So the question is, we know Cassady and Rick were both targets of abduction."

"Rick first, Cassady second."

"But what if it was the other way around?" Tallon asked. "Sandia information is highly classified, right? So how was Rick Simmons found in the first place? What if they located him through his wife? What if she filled out the paperwork at Industrial Supplies and put down Rick Simmons and then listed his current employer as Rio Grande trucking?"

"That would mean that someone knew Rio Grande Trucking was actually Sandia."

They drove, and Tallon realized he was heading back toward Pauling's hotel.

"Holy shit," Pauling said as she continued to read on her iPad.

"What?"

"I found an old medical journal where Walker said he was developing a new method for treating exposure."

"Exposure to what?" Tallon asked.

Pauling looked at him.

"Nuclear radiation."

52

P auling's phone buzzed a block from her hotel. She glanced at it and then spoke to Tallon.

"Ok. My contact just sent me the address for Vanguard Holdings. It's west of here. Just beyond the abandoned gas station, not far from where Rick Simmons' body was found," she said.

"Let's go," Tallon said.

He turned the car and pointed it west.

"Why am I not surprised at its location?" Tallon said. "It always seemed odd that Rick's body and the gas station were in the same rough vicinity."

"Now we know why," Pauling agreed.

It took them less than fifteen minutes to get

there, but when they approached the entrance, several squad cars had the road blocked.

"Well, that's not a good sign," Tallon said.

"Someone else may have beaten us to the punch."

An unmarked sedan was there, too. Either undercover cop, or FBI, Pauling thought.

"No way to get around them," Tallon said. "I'm going to pull over and see if someone notices we're here."

He drove onto the shoulder and before he was able to put the Impala into Park, one of the plain sedan's car doors opened.

"Feebie alert," Pauling said as she and Tallon watched the car.

"It's that Ostertag," Tallon said.

Along with him, Pauling saw a woman. Tall, with the build of a former athlete.

"She's FBI, too. But not local."

Ostertag waved them out of the car.

Pauling approached them first.

"Pauling, I thought I told you to stay away from this case," Ostertag said.

"I have been," she said. "We were just getting some things from Cassady's office and they told us she might have something out at her company's holding company. That's why we're here."

"What a load of bullshit," Ostertag said.

"It's the truth," Tallon said. "Odd we should bump into you out here. What's going on?"

"And is this your boss?" Pauling asked, lifting her chin toward the woman.

"This is Agent Hess," Ostertag said. "By the way, they have your friend Cassady. Stashing her in Chicago didn't work out very well."

He wasn't being smug, but the criticism still stung Pauling.

She was about to answer when the sound of a chopper roaring in from the south interrupted her.

Sand kicked up around them.

"Let's go," Hess said. She looked at Tallon and Pauling. "You're coming, too."

53

"There's no way they have Cassady," Pauling said after she'd put on her headset.

"Nice job protecting your client," Hess answered, her voice dripping with sarcasm.

They were airborne and roaring to the west. Pauling wondered why they'd been brought aboard. Definitely against standard FBI procedure. But she wasn't going to point that out to anyone.

It looked like she was finally going to get to the bottom of who had killed Rick Simmons. And she couldn't help but wonder if a rendezvous with Jack Reacher was in her immediate future.

"You're in way over your head," Ostertag said. "You two have no idea what you're dealing with.

You really should have listened to my advice and gotten out of Dodge."

"What do you mean we're in over our heads?" Pauling asked. "We found out about Vance Walker. We know he used information from Cassady's personnel record to discover her husband was a driver for Sandia. He must have killed Rick in order to get his hands on some nuclear material. That's what he's all about, right?"

Ostertag glanced around from the seat in front of Pauling. "I'm impressed," he said. "You had part of it."

"They don't need to know anything else," Hess said. "They're here just so we can keep an eye on them."

"Bullshit," Tallon said. "We're in it this far. You might as well use us."

"Use you for what?" Hess said. "You've got an overblown sense of self-importance. Just shut up and enjoy the ride."

"I don't think so," Pauling said. "How's this? Vance Walker is an inventor," she said. "What if he developed a treatment for radiation exposure. In other words, in a nuclear blast, cockroaches and Walker's patients would survive. Maybe he even injected Cassady with his secret formula. How's that, Agent Hess? Am I close?"

Hess turned around and looked at her. "Not bad," she said. "But again, that's only part of it."

"So arrest him," Tallon said. "You keep talking like you're one step ahead of everyone, but it sure doesn't look like it."

"We were planning to," Hess said. "We had our eye on him but he proved to be a little more industrious than we realized. Turns out he'd built that underground complex back there and was doing all kinds of stuff. And then he whacked Rick Simmons and stole a truck full of nuclear material."

"Why? Did he run out of the stuff for his medical experiments?" Tallon asked.

Ostertag and Hess didn't answer.

Pauling suddenly knew why.

"Holy shit, he's going to set it off somewhere as a huge medical experiment, isn't he?" Pauling asked.

"Not quite," Hess said. "It seems Mr. Walker went from an interest in medicine to genetics."

"Like what? Starting a new race?"

"He may have a bizarre plan to set off a nuclear war and that way, only he and the people he's vaccinated will survive," Hess said. "He'll own everything, once everyone dies from the fallout. He'll be the king of the world. Or, at least, what's left of it."

"That's crazy," Tallon said. "Where is this bomb of his?"

"We think he's heading for Los Angeles," Ostertag said.

"Does he really think a nuclear bomb in L.A. will start World War III?" Pauling asked. "No one's going to believe that."

"Doesn't matter," Hess said. "He believes it will. And now we've got to deal with it."

"We've got an FBI SWAT team en route to where we're hoping to cut off the truck," Ostertag said.

"Let's get this party started," Hess said.

"There," Ostertag said.

A single Crown Vic was parked on the side of the freeway. Pauling estimated they were maybe a hundred or a hundred and fifty miles from Albuquerque. Which meant that Walker and his truck had gotten a couple hours head start on them. She was surprised they had come that close to their operational launch.

Pauling wasn't a big fan of coincidence.

Why had Walker pulled out just before they'd gotten there?

"It's about ten hours to Los Angeles from here," Ostertag said. "We're at the foot of the El Malpais Conservation Area. Nothing here. This is where we're going to stop the truck."

Hess had directed the chopper to fly far enough away from the freeway to avoid being seen by Walker and his convoy.

"Put her down!" Ostertag yelled to the pilot.

They landed and Pauling removed her headset. She followed Ostertag out of the chopper, with Tallon behind.

The chopper then took off and flew behind a line of mountains to the north. There was grit in Pauling's mouth and she spat it out. As the sound of the helicopter faded, it was met with silence.

Pauling wondered how everyone could be so sure of the truck's location if all of the GPS technology had been removed previously.

"Tell them what they need to do here," Hess said to Ostertag, gesturing toward Pauling and Tallon. "I'm going to call into the HazMat and SWAT teams and check on their status. They should be here within fifteen minutes."

Hess turned toward the Crown Vic and its driver, putting a cell phone to her ear.

Ostertag turned to Pauling and Tallon.

"You are to be witnesses only," he said. "You are not to engage in any–"

Suddenly, the front of his face exploded outward in a shower of blood and brain matter. He folded to the ground and Pauling was reaching for her gun when she froze.

Hess stepped out from behind Ostertag's fallen body with her gun raised, a small curlicue of smoke rising from the muzzle, now pointed directly at Tallon and Pauling.

"He was right," she said. "You are only to be witnesses."

The driver of the vehicle got out of the plain sedan. Pauling felt like she'd seen him before. Maybe one of the thugs who had tried to grab Cassady at her house. The one who'd taken a shot at her.

Pauling watched as he went to the back of the car and popped the trunk.

He hoisted Cassady out of the rear of the vehicle, none too gently. Her hands were tied behind her back, a piece of duct tape was across her mouth, and her feet were duct taped together, too.

At least she's alive, Pauling thought.

"Getting rid of evidence, I see," Pauling said to Hess.

"Sure. Loose ends aren't a good thing in this kind of situation," Hess said. "It should have been taken care of much earlier but we weren't exactly working with the A-team."

An off-road vehicle emerged from behind one of the towering sandstone cliffs. It drove toward them and Pauling knew who was in it before the vehicle stopped.

A tall bald man emerged from the front passenger seat.

He walked with an exaggerated posture, and wore gold-rimmed aviator glasses with yellow tinted lenses.

Vance Walker, Pauling thought

He looked like a delusional cyborg. His body was lean and taut, and he moved with the easy grace of an athlete. It reminded Pauling of someone.

And then it hit her.

"Do we have a little father/daughter reunion going on here?" Pauling asked. "How touching."

"You're fairly perceptive," Hess said. "I'm kind of surprised you were such a failure at the FBI. That place is full of simpletons. You should have fit right in."

"Spoken like Daddy's little girl," Pauling said.

"The SWAT team was a nice touch," Tallon said. "You've thought of everything, except this plan will never work. Your old man's a crackpot and you're brainwashed."

"We have thought of everything," Walker said. "And I consider the label crackpot to be a good one. We've got a truck full of goodies for the city of Los Angeles. They deserve it."

"How many millions are going to die because of your experiment?" Pauling asked. "Do you really think it's going to incite a war?"

Walker rolled his eyes.

"How many people will die?" Walker asked. "The answer to that question is whatever the number, it won't be nearly enough. Which is why this is only the opening salvo in the war to remake the world."

"And while you accomplished nothing at the FBI," Hess said to Pauling. "At least you're going to finally get the credit you deserve."

Pauling had a sudden, stunning revelation.

"You sent me the letter with Reacher's name on it, didn't you?" Pauling asked.

Hess smirked at her.

"You saw my file," Pauling continued. "You knew I had worked with Reacher previously. Why? Why did you lure me out here?"

"I needed someone to blame for all of these murders. And to generally fuck everything else up," Hess said. "You seemed perfectly qualified. A former FBI agent, a bit of a rogue. A private investi-gator. I knew if I brought you out here, I'd have another chess piece to play with. It worked perfectly."

"No one is going to believe you," Pauling said.

"Aw, were you hoping to roll around the hay some more with Reacher?" Hess asked.

Pauling felt her face burn.

Hess leaned forward and whispered to Pauling. "Yeah, that was in the file, too."

Walker stepped around Hess. The other man, the one who'd shot at Pauling in Cassady's house, had now walked up to them. He pushed Cassady toward them and leveled his gun at them.

"Ah, here we are," Walker said.

Pauling had heard a rumble in the distance and now the convoy arrived. A Crown Vic in front, followed by a semi-truck pulling an extra wide trailer behind it. On the trailer was a large metal shipping container.

Two men got out of the Crown Vic and walked toward them. One of them was very tall and Pauling remembered that Tallon had described one of his beating victims at the gas station as being of impressive height.

The tall man smirked at Tallon.

"Showtime," Walker said.

55

Rollins and Petrie had dismissed the other members of the team. Now, they were on a live video link with an Air Force base whose location had not been fully disclosed.

The footage was grainy, but then again, it was being beamed from a UAV tens of thousands of feet above where Pauling and Tallon now stood.

"She's gone rogue," Petrie said. "Final confirmation."

The shit had hit the fan once Hess had been in Albuquerque. After her initial check-in, she had stopped providing any updates to the team. They'd been able to track her movements, but all communication had ceased. There hadn't been time to send in a second team.

All they had managed to do was confirm with Ostertag that Hess was leading the operation, but had stopped short of asking him to intervene and update them on her behalf. It would have raised too many red flags.

Now, they realized their mistake.

"How? Why?" Petrie asked.

"Oh, we'll get to the bottom of that," Rollins said. "But we've got to move on this now. And move fast."

He spoke into the headset.

"Agent down," he said. "Recommend we strike now. That truck cannot be allowed to go anywhere."

Rollins listened to his military counterpart on the other end of the line.

"Confirmed. Contents of vehicle must not be agitated," he said.

Petrie watched the figures on the screen. It looked like there was movement and he stifled the urge to shout an alarm.

"Roger that," Rollins said into his headset.

He turned to Petrie.

"Warn Pauling," he said. "She's got an incoming in about ten seconds."

56

P auling felt the phone buzz in her pocket. They'd taken the guns but not her phone. And now, the three of them were separated from the main group. Walker and Hess had approached the big truck, while the man with the gun kept his distance from them.

Her phone buzzed again and she waited until the man with the gun wasn't looking at her.

She was able to glance at the screen.

There were only two words and the message had come from an area code she recognized as Washington, D.C.

The message was clear.

Drone. Incoming.

She glanced up at Tallon, who was watching

her. Pauling looked at the bluff where Walker had been hidden during Hess's ambush.

Pauling glanced back at Tallon and nodded.

She turned and began running for the bluff. Behind her, she knew Tallon would grab Cassady and follow.

Her feet dug into the sand and at any minute she expected a bullet in the back, between her shoulder blades.

She heard someone shout and Pauling glanced back over her shoulder.

Tallon was carrying Cassady like a sack of groceries, and running at an angle, cutting every five steps to throw off the aim of the man with the gun. Pauling pivoted and changed direction just as the shooter fired another round.

Sand kicked up in front of her.

Pauling hoped they wouldn't be too eager to pursue them. After all, the only thing in front of them was a vast stretch of sand. Dozens of square miles of nothing but parched desert.

There was another shot and more sand kicked up in front of Pauling.

"Quit shooting, just run them down, you moron," Pauling heard Walker yell.

An engine roared to life behind them, but the

bluff was less than a hundred yards away. Tallon passed her, which pissed off Pauling. Even worse, she could have sworn she saw him smile as he raced past her. An impressive feat considering he was carrying a human being under his arm.

Behind them, Pauling heard the sound of an engine grow louder. Since the desert was flat, with no obstacles to maneuver around, the driver could easily catch them. But not before they made it to the bluff.

But just then, Pauling heard the sound of a second engine. This one had a tone that was much softer, much slower, and quite distant.

Instantly, she knew what it was.

She'd spent some time overseas, and had seen, and heard, her fair share of drones.

The sound was unmistakable.

It was reminiscent of a distant lawn mower.

The sound grew and then she saw Tallon disappear behind the bluff and she followed. There was a large rock outcropping and Tallon must have recognized the sound, too, because he threw Cassady behind the rock and waited for Pauling, who dove in on top of Cassady and then Tallon landed on top of her.

Just in time.

An explosion shook the ground and instantly falling dirt and rock rained down upon them.

Pauling could hear Cassady screaming underneath her.

The sound of the drone was gone.

And so was the sound of the car behind them.

Silence.

57

They got to their feet and Pauling freed Cassady from her restraints.

"Wait here," Pauling said. Cassady was a wreck, with tears smearing the reddish sand on her face. She slumped over and leaned against the base of a boulder. Pauling figured she couldn't even stand if she tried.

"It's going to be fine," Pauling told her. "I'll be right back. I promise."

She joined Tallon at the base of the bluff, and they both readied themselves to see what damage had been done.

"I'm impressed, Pauling," Tallon said to her. "Calling in a drone strike? You've got some pull, don't you?"

"I wish," she said. "I would have called it in a lot sooner."

They came out from behind the bluff and saw that the car pursuing them, and its driver, were gone.

In its place was a wrecked, burning shell of metal. The smell of burned flesh filled the air, along with acrid smoke and burning fuel.

Just beyond the wrecked car was a grisly collection of body parts, scattered like they'd been spilled from above.

Pauling spotted what was left of Hess. She'd been ripped in two. Carefully, Pauling approached, knelt down and used her fingers to extract Hess's gun from its holster.

Someone behind her yelled and Pauling turned just as Walker leapt from the ground, his face a bloody mask, and raised a gun, pointed at Tallon.

But Tallon was already moving. He simply stepped inside Walker's outstretched arm and punched him in the throat. He followed that with a terrific blow, an elbow to Walker's jaw that made a horrible popping sound and then Walker sank to the ground.

Tallon caught his arm and pulled the gun from

his hand. Tallon checked the pistol and held it in front of him, looking off toward the shipping container still on the truck.

It was intact.

Pauling thought for a moment that Tallon was going to shoot Walker, but instead, he stepped back and turned to Pauling. "That was precise–"

Suddenly, a gunshot rang out and Tallon threw himself to the left, rolled and sprang to his feet, the gun held in front of him, his finger on the trigger.

Pauling looked and saw Cassady standing six feet away from Walker, whose bald head was now sporting a big hole from which blood was gushing. He sank to his knees, and then fell face-first in the sand.

Cassady had a gun in her hand, which she now looked at as if it was a foreign object someone had placed there.

Pauling figured she must have found it in the wrecked car. She'd probably gotten it from the driver, the man who'd held them briefly at gunpoint.

Pauling walked toward Cassady, who stared at the dead body of Walker.

Finally, Cassady spoke.

"That was for Rick," she said.

58

Tallon stood next to his vehicle. It was late, and he had given serious consideration to spending the night in Albuquerque and heading back home in the morning.

But he decided against it.

It had been a strange ride, and he was looking forward to getting back to "his" desert. The thought of running free and being lost in his own thoughts was highly motivating. He was anxious to get on the road.

He and Pauling had waited with Cassady for the Feds to arrive, as Pauling knew they would. It took about an hour of them waiting before it happened. Eventually, after some long hours being questioned, they were released.

Cassady had been taken to a local hospital and was under care for some minor bumps and bruises. A distant aunt had agreed to come and help her get back on her feet.

And now, Tallon was just waiting for Pauling.

They had come back to her hotel and she had run in to get something for him. Now, she came back out and walked over to where he had parked.

"Pauling," Tallon said, "You sure know how to show a guy a good time."

"I appreciate that," she said. Tallon again marveled at her voice. That low, jazz-singer-the-next-morning rasp that was incredibly sexy. This was now another job where he'd worked with her and hadn't been able to make any progress romantically.

Well, maybe next time.

"But honestly, what did you think?" she asked. "That I would call you in for a divorce case? A cheating spouse?"

"No, I figured it would be good. Just didn't think it would be on this scale," he answered.

"Here," she said. She handed Tallon a check. He didn't even look at it.

"Until next time?" he asked.

"Sounds like a plan," she said. He leaned in,

then, and kissed her. It was a hell of a kiss, the kind that made him wonder why he hadn't tried it sooner.

She must have read his mind because after, she said, "Well, I've got a flight to catch in two hours. Drive safely, Tallon."

He smiled at her. Those green eyes were something else. Next time, he'd be a little more bold.

"Later, Pauling," he said. "You know where to find me."

He drove away and saw her turn and walk back into her hotel.

That's a hell of a woman, he thought.

EPILOGUE

Two Days Later

NEW YORK WELCOMED her back with a mailbox stuffed with letters, an email folder full of messages, and an office in need of some fresh air.

Pauling was back on her regular schedule. She'd already worked out, gotten her coffee, and unlocked the office. She cracked a window and then attacked her mail with gusto.

She'd also put in a call to Cassady and spoken with the aunt as well as the doctor to make sure the young woman and her unborn baby were both doing fine. She would recover, and hopefully start putting her life back together.

Tallon had sent her a photo from the backyard of his house. It had been last evening, and there was a small fire in the fire pit, with a mountain range in the background framed by a beautiful orange glow from the setting sun.

It had been an invitation of sorts, and Pauling was giving it some serious consideration.

Once she was caught up with her various bills, purchase orders and invoices, she worked until her little red icon for unread email messages finally blinked off.

She was officially caught up.

With her desk clear, she brought out the folder with Reacher's name on it.

For a long time, she simply stared at it.

It was this cheap little folder that had started it all.

She'd definitely wanted to see Reacher again, but she wondered how much of that was leftover physical attraction. And curiosity.

Pauling considered that. It wasn't like she was a young twenty-something, looking for love. At this point, she had made some choices and was comfortable with the results.

But who really knew what was going to happen? What the future might bring?

It was like she had told Tallon, life was just full of surprises.

Maybe one of them would turn out to be Jack Reacher.

THE JACK REACHER CASES
(BOOK TWO)

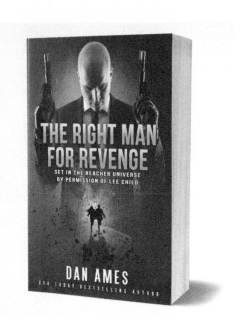

THE RIGHT MAN FOR REVENGE
A USA TODAY BESTSELLER

CLICK HERE TO BUY

FREE BOOKS AND MORE

Would you like a FREE book and the chance
to win a FREE KINDLE?

Then sign up for the DAN AMES BOOK CLUB:

For special offers and new releases, sign up here

ABOUT THE AUTHOR

Dan Ames is an international bestselling author and winner of the Independent Book Award for Crime Fiction.

www.AuthorDanAmes.com

dan@authordanames.com

ALSO BY DAN AMES

THE JACK REACHER CASES

The JACK REACHER Cases (The Man Who Works Alone)

The Jack Reacher Cases (A Man Built For Justice)

The JACK REACHER Cases #13 (A Man Born for Battle)

The JACK REACHER Cases #14 (The Perfect Man for Payback)

The JACK REACHER Cases #15 (The Man Whose Aim Is True)

The JACK REACHER Cases #16 (The Man Who Dies Here)

The JACK REACHER Cases #17 (The Man With Nothing To Lose)

The JACK REACHER Cases #18 (The Man Who Never Goes Back)

The JACK REACHER Cases #19 (The Man From The Shadows)

The JACK REACHER CASES #20 (The Man Behind The Gun)

JACK REACHER'S SPECIAL INVESTIGATORS

BOOK ONE: DEAD MEN WALKING

BOOK TWO: GAME OVER

BOOK THREE: LIGHTS OUT

BOOK FOUR: NEVER FORGIVE, NEVER FORGET

BOOK FIVE: HIT THEM FAST, HIT THEM HARD

BOOK SIX: FINISH THE FIGHT

THE JOHN ROCKNE MYSTERIES

DEAD WOOD (John Rockne Mystery #1)

HARD ROCK (John Rockne Mystery #2)

COLD JADE (John Rockne Mystery #3)

LONG SHOT (John Rockne Mystery #4)

EASY PREY (John Rockne Mystery #5)

BODY BLOW (John Rockne Mystery #6)

THE WADE CARVER THRILLERS

MOLLY (Wade Carver Thriller #1)

SUGAR (Wade Carver Thriller #2)

ANGEL (Wade Carver Thriller #3)

THE WALLACE MACK THRILLERS

THE KILLING LEAGUE (Wallace Mack Thriller #1)

THE MURDER STORE (Wallace Mack Thriller #2)

FINDERS KILLERS (Wallace Mack Thriller #3)

THE MARY COOPER MYSTERIES

THE CIRCUIT RIDER (WESTERNS)

THE CIRCUIT RIDER (Circuit Rider #1)

KILLER'S DRAW (Circuit Rider #2)

THE RAY MITCHELL THRILLERS

THE RECRUITER

KILLING THE RAT

HEAD SHOT

STANDALONE THRILLERS

KILLER GROOVE (Rockne & Cooper Mystery #1)

BEER MONEY (Burr Ashland Mystery #1)

TO FIND A MOUNTAIN (A WWII Thriller)

BOX SETS

GROSSE POINTE PULP

GROSSE POINTE PULP 2

TOTAL SARCASM

WALLACE MACK THRILLER COLLECTION

SHORT STORIES

THE GARBAGE COLLECTOR

BULLET RIVER

SCHOOL GIRL

HANGING CURVE

SCALE OF JUSTICE

Made in United States
Orlando, FL
23 June 2023

34445858R00168